Paradise Challenged

Johnny Gunn

Cover Art:
Michelle Crocker

http://mlcdesigns4you.weebly.com/

Publisher's Note:

This is a work of fiction. All names, characters, places, and events are the work of the author's imagination.

Any resemblance to real persons, places, or events is coincidental.

Solstice Publishing - www.solsticepublishing.com

Paradise Challenged
A Novel
By Johnny Gunn

Dedication

This book is dedicated to my lovely bride, Patty, in my full realization that it would never have come together without her trust and love.

Chapter One

"This trail couldn't get much colder, Sheriff," Red Feather said, as he tried to follow Thornton Holiday, gambler and murderer. "I'd call it off, myself."

The old man with a star under his heavy buffalo coat grumbled, spat some tobacco juice into the wind, and slumped into the saddle. "Yer right, damn it. All right boys," he said to the six-man posse, "let's go back. We've lost him. You'll all get your drink and cigar, even if we don't come in with the killer." The ride back was cold, wet, and somber.

Thornton Holiday, known for working near Salt Lake City with two other men had robbed banks in Wyoming Territory and Salt Lake City over a period of several weeks and had moved into Reno, Nevada. Between two banks, the three men had taken more than twenty thousand dollars in gold, silver, and paper money. On that last job in Reno, John Fowler was shot dead by a citizen as they were racing east out of town, and California Charlie, a half-breed killer was captured when his horse fell.

Holiday had timed the robberies to coincide with gold coin shipments from the mint in Carson City to the banks in Reno to await shipment to federal depositories by way of the Intercontinental Railroads, now open. Known for neither asking nor giving any quarter, Holiday was delighted that his two accomplices met their ends and he had massive amounts of gold in large canvas bags.

He had to get away from the posse that was sure to have formed, but equally important, he needed one or two pack animals. Between the large bags of gold, his own trail pack, and himself, he would destroy his horse in no time. Holiday was a large man, those who saw him were often intimidated just by his mean, nasty appearance, and he played up to the part.

He had few friends outside outlaw clans and gangs, but within were many that owed Holiday favors. He killed for necessity, and for pleasure, and those closest to him were kindred souls. *These heavy sacks of gold will set me up; I can feel my life's ambition coming true to my dreams. My town, my friends, safe from the law, under my watchful eye.* He pushed the horse as hard as he dared, and then, the rain and snow started falling.

The trail out of Reno followed the outlines of a wet swamp area people called the Truckee Meadows. Actually, considerable market hunting for water birds took place in the wetlands. The trail followed the Truckee River and the railroad tracks for more than twenty miles and then Holiday was in the great Nevada Desert.

The trail Holiday was using and the one the sheriff and his posse were floundering in had brought thousands of emigrants through these meadows on their great trek to the gold fields of California.

"Three days of rain, snow, and wind, and there just isn't a trail to follow," Red Feather said through clenched teeth. "Doubt that bastard will ever come back this way though. I'll give up today's hunt, Sheriff, but I'll have him in the back of my mind for a long time." Red Feather was well known in the law enforcement arena in the Great Basin and the loss of a man hurt.

He worked with sheriffs in Utah, Wyoming, Idaho, and Nevada, and Holiday had been in his sights for some time. "I've only lost a few, Sheriff, but this one is getting away mostly because of this foul weather." The sheriff was old and tired, would have given up the day before if it hadn't been for the tracker's insistence on following fragments of a trail. He just nodded, and the group returned.

Red Feather had a list he carried, and Holiday was close to the top. "My list of those I've lost over the years. Slowly, I'm afraid, but I am crossing off names, one at a time from that list." Thornton Holiday's name remained on the list.

Holiday made his way south, spending time in Arizona working on what he called, the finest plan any man could have. "I'm going to rule an area, like a king would, make my own rules, and bring as many of my friends as possible to work with me. My plan will work because I have enough money to make it work. Money, that's the answer, money is power, money will guarantee my plan."

That was how Thornton Holiday ended up in Plainsville, deep in the desert of New Mexico Territory on a bitter cold January morning, two large canvas bags well stowed on his pack mule, his duster tied to the back of the saddle. He was wearing a heavy Hudson Bay capote, with the hood pulled over his slouch hat; he rode a weary roan up to the livery.

It was well before sunrise and the stable boy noticed the man's horse was worn out, and his pack animal in worse shape. "Mornin'," the stable hand said, coming out of the barn. "'Bout the coldest wind yet this winter, I'm thinkin'. You all right, mister?" he asked, taking hold of the horse's headstall.

"Just cold and tired, boy." The big man, more than six feet tall and heavy in bone and muscle stepped slowly out of the saddle. He towered over the young stable boy, and jerked the two heavy bags off the mule. "Let 'em warm up a bit and catch their breath before you feed and water, boy."

Holiday untied his limited bedroll and kit from behind the saddle, stretched and shook like a spaniel, and spat a great wad of tobacco juice into the mud. "We've had a long ride. Where's the hotel?"

Joshua Pitts turned fourteen-years-old two weeks before stiffened when this huge man called him 'boy'. "I ain't a boy, mister. I'm fourteen, 'bout growed up," he snorted, leading the horse into the barn. "Hotel's down the street on the right," he called back over his shoulder.

Holiday chuckled, slung the heavy bags over his shoulder, and started off toward the main part of town. "Plainsville Hotel," he read as he got closer, "and right next door, the Red Rose Saloon. Hope there be good pickin's here." He had to ring the bell twice, slammed it hard the second time, before the desk clerk came out. Naturally angry at the world, holding his temper when dead tired and half frozen wasn't easy. "Took you long enough," he snarled.

Holiday pitched a double eagle at the man, said, "Room and a bath," as he signed the guest book.

"How long will you be with us, Mr. Holiday," the clerk said, glancing at the book.

"A few days, a few weeks, don't know, don't care."

"Take room 215, down the hall, second floor," he said, putting a big key on the counter. "Baths are in the back," and the clerk pointed down a hallway. "They won't open for business for a couple of hours. It's a separate business, so you will have to pay them at the time. Café will open shortly, through that door there, and the saloon is always open."

"You're one efficient little guy, eh?" Holiday chuckled. "Right now, all I want is a bed with warm blankets." He grabbed the key off the counter, slung his bags over his shoulder, and took the stairs at a slow clip. "This may be my new kingdom," were his last thoughts as sleep came on.

"I can't figure people out," the clerk muttered "One minute hard and angry, next making little jokes. He may have laughed a bit, but his eyes didn't. He's one mean son of a bitch," and the clerk went back to his little office. Holiday's intimidation factor worked on the clerk.

***

"Good morning, Mr. Sorenson. How was your night, not too busy I suppose?" The lady came through the hotel doors almost as a ray of sunshine, covered in a heavy coat with a floral print, fighting off a flurry of icy snow, carried by gale force winds. "No end to Mister Winter and his friend Jack Frost, eh? Young Mr. Pitts said a stranger rolled in early this morning, when I put up Beatrice and the buggy."

"Good morning, Mrs. Flannigan. Yes, and he's a big man," Gerald Sorenson, hotel clerk, said. "Looks like he might be a gambler, but he carries his sidearm like a gunman. Kinda low, and on the left side. He's in 215.

"Can I take your coat?" he asked, stepping from behind the counter. "Café's open, and it's a might warmer in there."

"Thank you, Gerald. I'll be in the office for a bit before breakfast, if anyone asks." Rose Flannigan purchased the hotel, café, and saloon when her husband, Horace, died and she came west with the proceeds from a thriving dry goods business in Missouri. She kept the name Plainsville Hotel and Café, but changed the name of the saloon to Red Rose Saloon and Dance Hall, the only saloon in town.

Plainsville was there because of neighboring ranches that raised fine beef and lamb. Corn grew well, and beans and squash. There was never a shortage of potatoes and onions, and much of it was transported east toward Santa Fé and Albuquerque, even into Texas, and south into Mexico. Cattle were driven to the major markets, north and east. Cattlemen in New Mexico Territory often still used the Goodnight-Loving Trail, at least as far north as Denver; many waiting for the Santa Fé line to come farther south.

Complaints of stolen cattle, shorted numbers at the rail-head, and other mis-appropriation of the herds were heard often. The trail originated years before when Texans began moving longhorns north, and Goodnight and Loving created their trail.

The produce was hauled out of town in large

wagons, headed often for Santa Fé, Albuquerque, and points in Texas. Those wagons returned with merchandise and supplies. Bill Pitts had room at his livery for all the large wagons, and featured ample sized corrals for the stock. Plainsville was an active little community.

Most of the ranches were remnants of the original Spanish Grants and many of the families were from Spanish ancestry, married into those moving into the territory from Texas. Mexicans and emigrants that had come west over the last two hundred years make up the rest of the population. The land was taken from its original Indian owners by the Spanish, then following the revolution, held by those claiming Mexican citizenship.

All of that changed following Mexican American hostilities and the Territory of New Mexico was formed from parts of Texas and the new lands from Mexico. Those ranching found a hard land, tough country in which to grow cows, and it took many generations to create what those in Plainsville have found to be good cattle country.

Rose Flannigan checked the register and noted the name Thornton Holiday written in a fine hand. "Must be an educated man," she mused as she walked down the hallway. Her offices were about half way down, with laundry facilities, the bathhouse, and barber-dentist shop taking up the end of the hallway. A doorway led to the carriage house at the back of the hotel, which hadn't been used much since the Pitts Blacksmith and Livery facility opened a few years ago.

Flannigan had thoughts of operating a small ranch when she first arrived in Plainsville, and homesteaded a hundred and sixty acres about seven miles east of the town. She found horrible weather, bad water, and more rocks than soil, and opted for being in the hotel business, but had made her home on the ranch, and drives her mare and buggy into town most mornings.

Rose worked at the books, a never-ending project,

what with several successful businesses, for three hours, emerged from her 'dungeon', as she called it, in time to join the late morning or early lunch crowd in the café. "Mr. Quimby, you're looking well, despite this cold storm that seems to have found a home in Plainsville. May I join you?"

"Absolutely, Rose," Pete Quimby said, standing and holding her chair. "Cold enough for you?" he joked. Pete Quimby owned the stockyards and the dry goods outlet, which serviced all the ranches in the area. Quimby moved to Plainsville from New Orleans several years ago and invested in the commercial interests in the community.

He said he made his money by moving cattle shipped to New Orleans from Europe. The cattle were then driven to ranches in Missouri and Texas. Tall and lanky, strong as any man in the area, Quimby took no guff from any man. He was fair in his business dealings and demanded fair treatment in return.

Ranchers in the area drove their market cattle to the stockyards, and when enough were on hand, were trailed to markets further east and north. Those companies that drove the herds out of the area were not always as scrupulous as Quimby, and the ranchers often complained about being shorted when the money was distributed.

Rose finished her scrambled eggs, smiled at the big man, and said, "Looks like Mrs. Jackson isn't having anymore trouble with her chickens laying in the winter. She must keep them warm or something. Best eggs we've had in a month.

"Oh, I say, who is that, just came in?"

Quimby turned to look back toward the door and saw a large, tall man in a black suit, white shirt with a string tie, and large revolver holstered just off his left hip. He wore a cropped head of curly black hair and had a pencil moustache, which set off large dark eyes covered in bushy black eyebrows. He appeared angry as he gave the room a look, walked over and sat at a table away from the front windows.

"That must be the stranger that Gerald told me about," Rose Flannigan said as Pete Quimby turned back to face her. "Young Joshua Pitts gave me a good description of the man also. Yes, he does look like a gambler, but also like a dangerous man."

"He's a gunslinger, alright," Quimby, said. "Wonder what brought him to Plainsville? Is he staying in the hotel?"

"Yes. Paid with a double eagle that he took from a large canvas bag he was carrying. Pitts said his animals were exhausted, so tired they didn't eat or drink, just stood in the warm stall and went sound asleep. Man shouldn't do that to an animal," she scowled across the table. "Maybe I'll just tell him so," she said, but with a smile, giving Quimby a sly little wink. More than one person could tell you about the Flannigan's Irish temper over the last few years.

"Might want to give that a second thought," he snickered back. Despite the humor in the words, Quimby continued, "I see a dangerous man with burning anger written across his face. It doesn't look like he knows anyone in the café, Rose, yet he's as angry a man as I've seen in a long time. It makes you wonder if he is capable of having a friend, or if he does, what would his friends be like?

"You have a terrible temper," he laughed, "but that isn't what drives your personality. You're fun loving, enjoy life, give people pleasure because of your friendship, and what I see over there," and he nodded his head, "is just the opposite. What makes people like that?"

"It's way too early in the morning to get into this kind of conversation, Pete," she said, giving him a beautiful smile. "You ponder those kinds of questions all by yourself, my friend. I'll worry about hotels, cafés and saloons."

She's a beautiful woman, he thought, looking deep into her blazing green eyes. *I wonder why she hasn't married up with one of the ranchers or businessmen in town? She would be a catch for a gentleman. I'm not old enough or wise enough, maybe not even good enough for her, but she would be a catch.*

"I better get over to the yards," Quimby said. "We might get that rail spur yet, Rose. I'm meeting with some of the ranchers and a representative of the railroad today. Our ranchers would increase their herds ten-fold if they could get them straight to the slaughter houses."

"That would be so good for them and for the town, Pete," she said. "Just imagine what a railroad would do for this area. Merchandise of every kind could be available to us, brought in fast and for a reasonable fare. I can see nothing but economic growth for the whole area. For what it's worth, Pete, make sure the ranchers and the railroad people know I'm in favor.

"Good luck with it. Drinks later?" she asked, and got a positive answer.

Quimby took his leave as well, and walked back to the feedlots through the gathering storm. *Gunslinger sitting in the Plainsville Café,* he thought. *Didn't think I'd see something like that this morning. Wonder what would bring an outlaw here? No bank to rob, no herds to rustle, no known gunman to fight.* He let the thoughts trail off, but they came back several times as the morning wore on.

***

Holiday was seen all over Plainsville during the following days, often at the telegraph office, sometimes at the stockyards, and daily at the café and Red Rose Saloon. "Doesn't have much to say," Quimby noted one night, standing at the long plank with John Morton, one of the ranchers, and Rose Flannigan. They watched Holiday come in the doors. "He's a strange one."

"One thing, though," John Morton said, "He understands why we want that railroad. Said a town our size and with all the outlying ranches, a railroad would be excellent.

"He's got a quick temper. Had words with old Charlie Sloan when Sloan's horse gave a little dance the other day. Got in his way, I guess."

"He's had words with Gerald Sorenson at the hotel, as well," Rose said. "Doesn't seem to like anything, but has questions about the economics of the town. You don't suppose he's here to rob the businesses, do you?" She shook her head at the question, and they continued to watch the newcomer.

Holiday strode to the bar, ordered a glass of whiskey and wanted a cleaner glass than had been offered. Old Pete, long time bartender at the Red Rose, and always one to grumble, stepped back and looked at the glass, snorted, and got Holiday another. He was called Old Pete to separate him from Pete Quimby.

"You wouldn't last ten minutes if I owned this piece of filth saloon," Holiday said, as he poured a healthy shot.

"Well, you don't, Mr. Holiday, I do," and Rose Flannigan got right in his face. "If you don't like it here, go somewhere else, or build your own saloon." The Irish went more than skin deep, surfaced at the slightest test, and Holiday had struck a chord. "All you've done since arriving here is complain about the bedding, complain about the heat, and now complain about the glasses. I understand the coffee wasn't up to your standards the other morning.

"Maybe you'd be happier somewhere else."

"You're right, lady," he snapped, slamming the empty glass on the wood plank. He had a menacing look smeared across his broad face. "Maybe I would," and he seemed to make the slightest move toward her. Quimby tightened up for a fight, Old Pete stepped close to the shotgun he had handy under the bar, and Rose Flannigan held her ground.

At the last second, Holiday turned and glared at Old Pete, gave the bar a sneer, and swaggered out the doors. One could feel the tension lift. "Don't serve him again, Pete," Rose said. "His room at the hotel is paid through tomorrow night, so I can't do anything about that, but I'll not let him stay any longer. You were right, Pete. He's dangerous."

She motioned to set up the house, which brought cheers from the gang when Old Pete rang the bell behind the bar. "He hasn't caused any trouble yet, Pete, but I can almost feel it coming. Mighty quick to complain, mighty quick to anger, I think. Well, that said, how did your meeting with the railroad people go the other day. Haven't had a chance to talk about that. Hell, boy, haven't seen you around much."

"Been busy, Rose. We did have drinks and dinner the other night, though." She nodded and smiled at that, and Quimby continued. "The main line will remain north of us, but the old man," and he paused, trying to remember his name, then said, "Shelby, that's it, Myron Shelby, said he's put a survey crew out to run that spur to Plainsville. We'll be shipping cattle out of here in railcars, Rose."

John Morton, smiled, said, "I've been running a small herd simply because I'm not set up for those long drives north. I've had to join with other small ranchers on the drives, and we are all sure that we've taken it bad from those bamboozlers. Ship out fifty head, get paid for thirty. Bah.

"Now, I can increase my productivity, hold back heifers year in and year out, build a big herd, and ship right out of Pete's stockyard."

"That's right, John. I'll buy everything you bring me, at a damn good price, and fill those boxcars. Those folks back east are gonna be eatin' good when that spur is in."

Chapter Two

Holiday spent great amounts of time at the telegraph office, and some in town were more than just interested, including Sheriff Rudy Thomas. "Quimby, we need to talk," Thomas said, meeting him in the street one day. "This Holiday feller has been sending a lot of telegraph messages all over the west. Old Tater isn't supposed to say what they are, but he told me."

"Our upstanding lawman is breaking the law, Sheriff?" Pete joked, as the two walked into the Plainsville Café. "But I have to admit, I'm interested in knowing, too. That man scares me."

"The messages are going to men and women that I know are outlaws. He's inviting them to join him here in Plainsville. In one, I remember, he said, 'the pickin's are good.' That's what he said. He's up to something."

They were at a table for six near the back of the café, close to the kitchen and its warmth, watching out the window as another major winter storm tore up the countryside. "Winds are fierce this time, Pete. Took out the livery stable sign this morning. Old Pitts will have kindling for his fires for a while."

Dave Peterson, rancher and part-time cobbler joined them. "Hear the latest on Holiday?" he asked, pulling out a chair. "Bought those two empty lots down near the stables. Told Jesse Cooper he's gonna build a fancy saloon and gambling hall. Told Jesse he would hire him."

"I wonder if Rose knows that," Quimby said. "I better let her know. She's sure Cooper has been holding out on her." Cooper ran the only gambling table in Plainsville. He started to get up when Rose Flannigan came into the restaurant and headed straight for their table.

"You hear the latest?" she said, letting Pete Quimby hold her chair. "That Holiday is going to build a saloon, and he told Pitts he would put me out of business." The Irish was about to have a field day. "I've heard some real bad stories about that man in the last few days. Sheriff, what do you know?"

"I was telling Quimby here," Sheriff Thomas said, "that Holiday has been sending messages to bad men and gunslingers all over the west, saying the pickin's are good in Plainsville. Another rumor, Holiday was thrown out of Virginia City, way up north in Nevada. He's friends with crooked gamblers, card sharks, dice shavers, and gunslingers. I've sent some telegraphs as well, to some lawmen around. See if I can get a handle on the situation."

"You're a deep man, Pete," Rose said. "You've been around places. What makes a man like Holiday act the way he does? Where does a constant anger come from? I have a little bit of a temper," she said, guffaws sounded not just from their table, and she gave everyone a scowl, then brightened into a smile. "OK, maybe more than a little bit, but having a temper is different from being constantly angry."

"I have been thinking about that," Quimby said, his deep southern charm spreading around the room. Sitting up in his chair and reaching for a cheroot, he gave the impression of a rather young politician or orator. "There is a vast ocean of difference between he and I. I would think that something or someone hurt him deeply, years ago. I don't see where he has the least trust in anyone, including his closest associates, and with that anger and distrust comes danger. What would it have taken for him to have swung on you, the other night, or worse, shot you?" he said to Rose.

"I hope I'm not around to find out what the trigger would be," Quimby said. "His eyes never smile, and what's worse, he never looks you in the eye." He settled back in his chair, smiled just a bit and continued. "I would guess that he only has one true friend, and that would be himself.

"We've seen that he is very self-assured, swaggers about, but watches those around him, wanting to see a reaction, desperately needing assurance from others, and would not admit that if you were yanking his fingernails. He loves himself on the one hand and doubts himself on another and is terrified that someone will know that.

"That's where the anger comes from. He believes he is better than everyone else and then is wracked with self-doubt."

"As I said, Pete," Rose Flannigan said, leaving the café, "You're a deep man."

***

Holiday paid for his land with more of those gold coins, paid for everything with them, and before long wagon loads of lumber and other building material arrived in Plainsville. Locals chatted about progress on the new saloon comparing its size to that of the Red Rose. More were worried about Holiday's reputation. Holiday seemed to be his own job site foreman, but the man that caused the most trouble with the workers was Mike Middleton, a newcomer, apparent good friend to Holiday.

Middleton had a bad scar down the length of his face, from the middle of his forehead, across his nose and cheek, ending somewhere under his shirt. His eyes were set close together, just small slits, and coupled with a mouth that featured thin lips and a constant grimace, Middleton gave the appearance of a snake, a rattler, ready to strike at any moment. His temper fluctuated from angry to incensed, and no one ever heard the man laugh or joke around. He drank strong liquor, used foul language without regard to who might hear him, and seemed to have a natural hatred toward children.

If youngsters were playing near the job site, he chased them off using horrible language. Women and men were complaining to the sheriff regularly about the beast of a man and his treatment of children.

Those near the construction site heard his booming voice as he berated the carpenters and workers in language unfit for genteel society. One day, most of that end of the village heard an argument between Iron Mike and Bill Pitts. "Middleton, quit cursing like that. There are women and children around," Pitts yelled at him from the livery stable.

"Mind your own business, blacksmith, and while you're there, go to hell," followed by a volley of increasingly bad language. "What are you looking at, pecker head?" he howled at a worker. "Get your ass back to work."

Middleton wore out his welcome at the Red Rose within days of his arrival. He pulled a gun on Old Pete and tried to hustle a couple of the local women, even while their husbands were there, and often referred to himself as Iron Mike. Sheriff Rudy Thomas ushered him out of the saloon and threatened to put him in jail if he pulled a gun on an unarmed man again.

"You take that little tin badge off, old man, and I'll whup you bloody and dead. Or better, draw on me, oh mighty shereef, and I'll put two slugs through your heart before your iron feels your hand." Middleton vowed to anyone who would listen that he would kill the sheriff and anyone who would stand with the sheriff.

Middleton had the size and strength to carry off the continual bullying. People in the community complained to Rose Flannigan, complaints were made to the sheriff, and Quimby had visitor after visitor at the stockyards, discussing the problems that were swirling around the town.

"I know Holiday is working from some kind of plan," Sheriff Thomas said one day as he and Quimby were walking through the corrals and pens at Quimby's stockyards, "but just what it is I can't figure out. We don't have a bank he could rob; we don't have any major businesses that he could rob. What is this outlaw gang up to?"

Holiday had enough of the building up within a week to actually open, although customers had to fend about through the construction. Jesse Cooper quit the Red Rose and opened his gambling tables at what Holiday was now proclaiming to be Hearts of Gold Saloon and Pleasure Palace. He hired Iron Mike Middleton to keep the peace, three men who had personal knowledge of the inside of the Plainsville jail were brought on as bartenders, and word was spread that several working ladies would be arriving as soon as the upstairs bedrooms were finished.

Sheriff Thomas, John Morton, and Pete Quimby, decided it was probably time for them to visit this new pleasure palace and see just what Holiday was up to. They had been drinking at the Red Rose. "It is possible that we've been wrong about the man," the sheriff said.

"I don't think so," Quimby said. "That Mike Middleton has a bad reputation, not wanted I guess, at least that we know of. Cooper is a thief, and all of the rest of his staff have spent time in your jail. If he brings trouble to the community, it could end our chances of getting that railroad spur. All they're doing right now is preliminary surveying; it isn't a done deal yet."

They walked up the street and turned the corner at the livery stable. "Look at that," Morton said, pointing at the new building. "That's one big building. Enough lights to keep old Bernie buying kerosene by the railcar, when the trains come." There was irony buried deep in the humor.

There was a hum of activity when they entered and walked to the bar. Frank Colter, recently a visitor to Thomas's jail was behind the bar. "How about a bottle and three glasses, Frank," Quimby said, admiring the back bar that had arrived on a wagon just a day or two before. "Wonder where Holiday found that back bar? Beautiful wood work, for sure."

"You brave enough to wear that star?" a voice loud

enough to be heard above the crowd, said. Thomas, Morton, and Quimby turned, and came face to face with Mike Middleton. The foul mouthed and angry man stood back about ten feet, his legs were slightly spread, hands hung loose at his side. He was wearing a gunfighter's rig, slung low on his right hip, the holster filled with a large revolver.

"I'm Rudy Thomas, Sheriff of this town, Mr. Middleton. I don't take kindly to threats, or being pushed around. Are you threatening me? Because if so, I will have to arrest you. We don't cater to loud mouth bullies around here."

Middleton's right hand was fast, Thomas's right hand was fast, and the two guns exploded almost simultaneously, both men flung backwards from the shock of large lead bullets. Blue smoke filled the air followed by silence. Not a sound, no dice thrown, no raises at the card tables, no dancing girls' trills of laughter.

Thomas took a round through his left shoulder, bones shattered, muscle and flesh ripped and torn. Middleton took one through his right arm, just above the elbow, the chunk of lead smashed the bone into splinters, his arm was bent in different directions. Both men were on the floor as blood puddled and smoke slowly cleared.

Morton and Quimby had their weapons drawn and Cooper decided against going for his while Frank Colter just stood behind the bar, being very quiet. "Somebody get the doc," Quimby demanded as Holiday came down the wide staircase from the second floor. Two men ran out the door for the doctor as Thomas and Middleton slowly bled, both near death.

"What the hell's going on?" Holiday demanded, kneeling at Middleton's side. "Colter, throw me a towel, quick, damn it." He stuffed the towel around the wound, stemming the blood. Morton was beside the sheriff, using the lawman's coat to help slow the blood.

"Your man Middleton challenged the sheriff, Holiday," Quimby said, his revolver still in his hand. "If he survives, he'll spend some time in the Plainsville jail. First the threat, then tried to draw first. Is this what our town can expect from the people you hire here, Holiday?"

"Get the hell out. You're not welcome here," Holiday exploded, but did not go for his own weapon; saw Quimby's already in hand. He was shaking with anger, his eyes were narrowed to slits, and his hand, so close to the butt of that revolver.

"Not 'till the doc gets here," Quimby said. "Let's everyone calm down. There's no reason for anymore gunplay. Ah, here's Doc Winters now." Slowly the crowd went back to the bar, to the gambling tables, the piano man's fingers danced, and so did the girls, now with slightly subdued humor. The two wounded men were carried to Winters' offices next to the Plainsville Hotel. He shooed everybody out, and he and his wife, Anna, also his nurse, started cleaning up the bloody mess.

Quimby found Rose, helping to close up the restaurant and brought her up to date. "Doc is going to need some help, Pete. I'm going over there," she said. "Is this the start of the trouble we've been expecting? Holiday has trouble written all over him." Quimby walked her to the door and went down the street to find Bill Pitts, the owner of the livery stable, but also Rudy Thomas's only part time deputy sheriff.

"Pitts," he said. "I've got bad news. Rudy has been shot and is in critical condition. I'm afraid your part time status just got changed."

"Damn. What happened? It's hard enough doing just part time for Rudy. I've been begging him to hire a full time deputy. Who shot him?"

Quimby spent the better part of an hour bringing Pitts up date on what had been going on in the town. "With all my blacksmith work, caring for all these horses, and calls to the ranches, I just don't get around town much. I'll do what I can, Pete, but we will need Rudy back on the job just as soon as possible."

***

"He's not going to make it, Rose," Doc Winters said, as he washed his hands for the tenth time, and applied more dry dressing to the sheriff's badly torn up shoulder. "He's lost so much blood, that bullet did so much damage. One little move and he'll start to hemorrhage again. All I can do is try to keep him quiet and hope for the best." He took a seat at his desk in the office, offered a chair to Rose, and rested his chin in his hand.

"Mr. Middleton will live, but I had to take off the bottom half of his arm. The bullet shattered the elbow and the arm couldn't be saved. He actually threatened us," he said, shaking his head. "But there wasn't anything else I could do. He's sedated right now, but I don't know what's going to happen when he wakes up."

"I'll go find Pete. Maybe he can get Holiday to move Middleton to his place before he comes to." She left and bumped into Holiday coming to see the doctor. "Mr. Holiday, I was just going to find you. Mr. Middleton will live, but Doctor Winters had to remove part of his arm.

"He's sedated right now, but was in a rage earlier. Can you and your men move him to your place."

"And your tin-horn sheriff? He gonna live?" Holiday barked, brushing past her.

"Maybe not, which might not be good for your man," she said, her Irish up and continued to glare at the man. She walked on out to the sidewalk expecting to get shot in the back and turned next door to her hotel and office. "Mr. Sorenson, I'm glad you're already on duty. I'll be in my office, and will probably take a room upstairs rather than try to get back to the ranch tonight.

"Unless it's urgent, please don't bother me. I'm exhausted," and she took a key to a room and walked back

23

to her office.

***

On the third day following the shooting, Sheriff Rudy Thomas died. Bill Pitts tried his best, but being full time deputy wasn't going to work. It was interfering with his business. "Please do something, Pete. You're the closest thing we have to a city official even if Plainsville isn't a real city."

"We have a meeting with the railroad tomorrow morning, Bill, and I'll get something done right after that. You've done a fine job in a tough situation. Just hang on for a little longer." Quimby was working to get a citizens' committee established to create, as Pitts called it, a real city.

"We need a town council, Bill, we need rules and laws so we can grow, economically and legally. You've been saying it, I've been saying it, and it's time to quit talking and get to work. With the railroad hopefully coming, with Holiday and his bunch of hooligans, we are gonna need some strong law enforcement." He shook his head and continued. "Maybe I'll just simply call for a meeting of everyone during our meeting with the railroad tomorrow."

The railroad had called the meeting, which also worried Quimby. The shooting, the men Holiday was bringing to town, and now Thomas's death might not go over well with the railroad. "I'll need your help, Bill, but we can call for some of the people to get together and lay out what our little town should be. We need elections for official positions, particularly sheriff, and get some real laws on the books."

"Well, do your best until we can get you some help. See you at the meeting."

***

Sheridan George rode into the sleepy little village late that night, covered in trail dust. A howling, icy wind blew his long red beard, forced his duster to whip about, which revealed an ornate revolver on his left hip. There was a carbine in its saddle scabbard and a bedroll tied to the back of his saddle.

Sheridan George was a block of muscle. He stood about five feet ten inches and weighed around two hundred pounds, and as early risers noted, he sported a broad nose made wider by more than one fist in his history.

Unlike most coming in from days on the trail, George did not take his horse and pack mule to the livery for feed and water, did not pull up at the Plainsville Hotel for a room and a bath, but rode straight to the Hearts of Gold Saloon and simply stepped off his trail weary horse, and tied it off. He kicked trail dust off his boots, dusted off his large sombrero, and swaggered into the busy saloon.

Three men at the bar moved aside to give the big man room. "Whiskey," he said, angry eyes glared at the young man behind the oaken plank. "Where's Holiday?"

"Mr. Holiday isn't here. It's late."

"Get him," is all George said, and when the bartender didn't move instantly, George's right hand shot out and grabbed him by the shirtfront. "Get him now, boy," and he lifted him over the bar and slapped him hard across the face, and shoved him toward the door.

"He lives upstairs," the young bartender whined. "I'll get him."

"Kind of rough on the kid, weren't you?" one of the men at the bar said.

"You don't like it, do something about it. Or mind your own business," he growled, as he spun around to face the man, his hands near his sides. The man turned fast, pulled iron as he did, and was thrown back ten feet from the force of a .40 caliber piece of hot lead as it passed through his heart.

There was dead silence again in the large barroom as the smoke began to clear and Sheridan George simply reached across the bar for a bottle of whiskey. Within a minute Thornton Holiday came down the large staircase from rooms on the second floor of the building. "Well I'll be damned," he said. "Sheridan George, you got my message. The dead man was one of my best, Sheridan."

"Then your best is piss poor, Holiday. What's so important I had to leave Tombstone?"

"Come upstairs, we'll talk. No, leave the bottle, I've got good stuff up there," he laughed, stepped over the dead man and shook George's hand. "Some of you boys take care of Jacobson. Good to see you, George."

***

Ralph Flowers, one of the Railroad's managers, brought a couple of other people with him for the meeting with Quimby and members of the Plainsville business and ranching community. Quimby brought things to order and introduced Flowers, a stern looking man who seemed to spend a great deal of time outside an office. He was deeply tanned, trim despite nearing what might be considered middle age, and wore a gun belt that was obviously handmade, with leather tooling and intricate silver work.

"Well, Mr. Quimby, citizens of Plainsville, I'll get right to the point. The railroad has some serious questions regarding putting a spur line into this community. The criminal element is one of our concerns," which brought Holiday to his feet.

"I don't feel there's a criminal element in Plainsville, sir." His eyes narrowed at the comment from Flowers, his hand visibly shaking with anger.

"We do, and that's what matters, Mr. Holiday. Two shootings in your saloon inside of a week, two men dead, and a town of only a few hundred people? You, sir, seem to attract an element the railroad is not comfortable with.

"Also, with the death of your sheriff, the town has no full-time law enforcement."

"I've put a lot of money and time into this forlorn

little village," Holiday said, glaring about the room. "Ignorant people for the most part," he said, giving Pete Quimby a hard look. "That's why I've had to bring in my own people. To run things properly."

Flowers was visibly taken aback by the outburst and Quimby was thinking that one more comment like that last one, and there would be one hell of a fight. "That kind of talk is uncalled for, Mr. Holiday," Flowers said. "The people of Plainsville are far from ignorant, and the economic possibilities of the area are great. That's why we want our railroad spur to come through. Another outburst like that and I'll leave for Santa Fé immediately and cancel all work on the spur."

Quimby wondered if Flowers had gone too far; would Holiday respond with violence? The almost leader of the town spoke up, "One of the things on today's agenda, Mr. Flowers, is a call for an election, and a new sheriff. We will see to it that he also has a full-time deputy."

"That's good, Quimby. That's good. The other matter is the economic stability of Plainsville. There is no bank in town, therefore no business or property loans, and this is of grave concern to us. As I understand it, Mrs. Flannigan at the Plainsville Hotel does make a few small loans, and does keep some of the businesses' extra money in her safe.

"For this community to grow, which it needs to do to support a rail line into town, there must be a banking enterprise of some sort."

"I can answer that," Holiday spoke up, his anger somewhat subsided. "An acquaintance from Virginia City, currently the chief clerk at the Bank of California, has been looking to establish a bank of his own. He has all the necessary backing and financing for such an enterprise. I have invited him to look over Plainsville.

"I'm not pleased with having to put any money of mine in my competitor's safe. In fact, I won't."

The meeting went on for another couple of hours, Flowers and Holiday sniping a bit, but tempers held in check. Later that evening, at supper in the Plainsville Café, Flowers sat with Quimby and Rose. "I've heard nothing but bad reports on your Mr. Holiday, Quimby. I'll bring the report from today's meeting back to the board of directors, and I hope you can find a way to control what I consider a bad situation."

"Another desperado came to town last night or early this morning, and one of Holiday's own henchmen was killed," Rose Flannigan said. "I don't like that man, and worse I'm afraid of him."

"Keep me informed, Quimby. Mrs. Flannigan, good evening. We'll be checking out very early for the ride back to the railhead. We want this spur, you need the spur, but there are serious dangers."

"I think the election for sheriff will change a lot of things, Flowers. Have a safe trip back." The railroad man went upstairs to his room and Quimby and Rose walked into the Red Rose for a nightcap.

"I'm going to run for sheriff, Rose. I'm big and strong, good with a gun, fair with people, and the people in town trust me. I think it's the right thing to do."

"You've sure got my support, Pete," she said, as she patted him on the shoulder. "It's an awfully dangerous job, and honestly, I wouldn't want to lose one of my best friends."

***

Quimby stayed up late, worked for hours at his desk in the stockyard. *I've never contemplated being a sheriff or any kind of lawman, but what's happening here must be stopped,* he said to himself. *What is Holiday's plan? What is he going to gain by killing people and taking their property? It can't be the property he wants, it must be something else.*

Quimby liked to think he was intelligent, had the

ability to reason out problems, and was baffled by Holiday and what was taking place in Plainsville. If a man operated a successful business, he believed, he would want the railroad to build a spur to the town, he would want a bank to support businesses and ranches, and he would want strong law enforcement. That same man, Quimby was thinking, would not in turn kill and steal, for some reason that just doesn't make sense.

"Holiday is working at cross purposes," Quimby said right out loud, staring into the fire burning hot on a long cold night. The large man stood up, poured a glass of brandy, and stood in front of the fireplace. *The man must be mentally unstable, seems willing to take by force what he could simply acquire legally with little effort.* The one sided conversation continued well into the early hours of the morning.

He drafted a plan that he would present to the next public meeting, a plan that called for Plainsville to declare itself a township, either by way of the territorial government or a county entity. He laughed at himself, thinking, *I don't know which. I don't even know if there is a county. Maybe that's why Holiday picked Plainsville. There is no legal entity to challenge him.* The people of Plainsville would create a town government with an elected council, and specific laws under which the people of the town would live.

The document was several pages long, detailed, and specific in its intent, and Quimby felt it answered many of the problems that Plainsville was experiencing. "This should be acceptable to the railroad people as well," he said, holding it up to read aloud again, pacing around the office. *I'll let Rose read this, and then call for a public meeting to present it. I think right after the election will be a good time to put this together.* He was smiling for the first time in many hours as he blew out the lanterns, banked the fire, and found his way to the bedroom.

***

"Looks like your call for an election for sheriff has people nicely stirred up, Pete," John Morton said, as he sat down for breakfast. "Saw your poster up at one of the hotel's windows, and I think I saw another one at the livery. Don't know if you really had to spend money on posters. You should just walk right in to that office."

Pete Quimby sat back, chuckling a bit. "Don't be counting those chickens yet, John. But I do want the job. Plainsville can become a nice little town for us, there's economic opportunity here, John. We need to keep the town safe, make families feel safe, and not let Holiday and his riff-raff have the run of the place.

"Well, how's that for my first political speech?" he said, but one could see the seriousness of the matter as his eyes narrowed slightly, not filled with humor. "According to Rose, and she knows these things, we have to have the notice of an election posted for thirty days before the election, so that notice went up yesterday. Looks like the election will coincide with the arrival of spring."

"I'd call that a good omen," Morton said.

Chapter Three

On the third day following the notice of election, a new set of posters was seen on every post and open site throughout Plainsville. Sheridan George was running for sheriff against Pete Quimby. Iron Mike Middleton was helping him put the signs up. Along with that, Holiday had purchased another lot on the main street and was in the process of putting up a structure.

"What's he building now?" Rose asked Quimby, sitting down to breakfast. "Looks substantial, anyway."

"According to young Joshua Pitts, it's the new bank building. Josh said a man named Henry Swanson arrived yesterday, and will open his bank as soon as the building is completed. That kid seems to know everything that goes on around here," he joked. "Apparently Swanson does have that financial backing Holiday talked about, at least according to rumor by way of the telegraph office.

"Well, I have to get back to the stockyard. I've got new posters coming in and need to get them up. This guy George is an ornery bastard. Bill Pitts caught him taking one of my signs down and putting his up. Guess it almost got nasty. Keep your eyes open," and he left the café. Rose took a walk down to the livery.

"Hi, Josh. Looks like you've been busy around the stables."

"Good morning, Mrs. Flannigan. Yes, with dad being a full time deputy, I've been doing most of the work. I'm getting pretty good at making horseshoes. That hammer sure is heavy, though. I guess that's why dad is so big." He was putting iron nails into kegs, and slamming the lids into place. "Mr. Holiday ordered another three hundred pounds of nails, so I've really been busy.

"Is Mr. Quimby going to be Sheriff? That Mr. George is not a nice man. Dad caught him ripping up one of Mr. Quimby's posters. I don't like him."

"That's part of what I want to talk to you about, Josh. Pete's going to need all the help he can get to win, and I think you can help. Just keep your eyes open and let your dad know if you see something wrong going on. And, let me know also. Can you do that?"

"Oh, yes, I can do that. That Mr. Middleton is awfully mean to his horse, and has a hard time saddling and bridling him, now that he only has one arm. I offered to help, and he tried to hit me. I'm quick though. But, instead, he hit his horse. That's not right."

"No, it isn't, Josh. Mr. Quimby and I need your help, so don't get hurt," she said, and gave the boy a big smile. She walked back to her office with worry written across her pretty face. *Grown men, one armed or not should not try to hit little boys and should never hit their horse,* she said to herself, angry at what the boy had said.

Josh spent the next several minutes making plans. *There are ways around this town that most of the adults don't know a thing about. I'll see to it that Mr. Quimby and Mrs. Flannigan know who is doing what, in particular that Mr. George.*

***

"Hey, you," Gerald Sorenson yelled, running out the front door of the Plainsville Hotel. "Leave that sign right where it is. You don't have any right to take it down. Leave it alone."

"Shut up, you little pipsqueak, or I'll nail you up here," Mike Middleton laughed, joined by George, ripping Quimby's sign off the hotel post and flinging it at the clerk. "You don't like it, do something about it, shorty," and Middleton put a fist in the clerk's face, knocking him back into the side of the building.

Two men in the street came forward, one trying to get Sorenson up on his feet, the other yelling at George. "You two are out of line. How dare you take Pete's poster down. I'll certainly never vote for someone with no morals." George grabbed the man by the throat and threw him into the muddy street.

"You ever talk to me like that again, and you'll be dead," he said, drawing his revolver and shooting two rounds into the mud near the unarmed man. Dan Jenkins, owner of the Plainsville Emporium jumped to his feet, and with George laughing, ran to his shop, two doors down from the hotel. Two more shots rang out, splattering mud at the man's feet.

"When I'm sheriff, you people better show a little more respect," he laughed, dumping the empty brass in the mud and reloading the weapon.

At the sound of gunfire, several people came out from shops and stores, and Pete Quimby came running up the street from the stockyards. "What's going on?" he asked, spotting his ripped up election poster and Gerald Sorenson standing on shaking legs, nursing a bloody nose.

"He ripped your sign down," Sorenson whined, pointing at Mike Middleton. "And George tried to shoot Mr. Jenkins."

Quimby spun on Middleton and George. "You rip another sign down and I'll file charges. That's a serious charge, and certainly not one that someone who wants to be sheriff should consider. You're not qualified to be sheriff, George. You're nothing but a damn criminal yourself, and you, Middleton, you're already facing murder charges.

"You'll be arrested the second I'm elected. Now, clear off, get out of here," and he stood facing the two, arms hanging nice and loose, ready for whatever happened next. People on the street moved away from the three men, out of the way of whichever way bullets might fly. Sorenson slipped into the hotel to find Rose Flannigan.

"What's going on? Who was shooting?" Bill Pitts was running up the street, still wearing his blacksmith chaps, and he had his gun out. He saw the ripped up election poster on the ground, saw Quimby and George faced off and ready to shoot each other.

"George, Middleton, you rip off another election notice? Did you?" he demanded, glaring at the two.

"Go to hell," Sheridan George said, spun around, and walked toward the Hearts of Gold Saloon. "Come on, Iron Mike, we've got work to do."

Quimby, Pitts, and several other people just stood there, as the two walked away. "Should have arrested them, Pitts," was all that Pete Quimby said as he turned on his heel and stalked back to the stockyard.

***

"You're not helping yourself, doing things like that, Sheridan," Thornton Holiday said, pouring drinks. "We need you to win this election for our plans to work. We'll never pull it off if Quimby wins. Now, back off on the bull headed stuff. Once you're the sheriff, and Swanson has his bank open, we will begin to make more money and have more power than you've ever dreamed."

He looked at the stocky man and asked, "Do you understand what real power is? Power, Sheridan, real power is control, and that's what we're working toward. I want control of this entire area, the town, the ranches, the people. What I say is law, George, what I demand will be done, and that's why you need to be sheriff." *Many towns and cities have mayors,* he mused, watching George, wondering if the big man was really the one for the job of sheriff. *Plainsville won't have a mayor. I think I'll call myself a Grand Duke. That's far more fitting for such a position by such a man.*

"Yeah, yeah," George said, and drank a healthy shot of fine bourbon and poured a second. The two were in a suite of rooms on the second floor of the new saloon, decorated in polished wood, nice carpet, and full liquor cabinet. "That little pisser of a hotel clerk started yelling, and Mike smacked him a good one, and things got started.

"I still don't understand that plan of yours, Thorny, but I'll quit messin' with people," and he growled, "ripping up posters."

"Right now, we need to concentrate on winning this election," Holiday said, again. "It's a small town, Quimby is well liked, and we have to win. No more of this nonsense. We are going to rule, I will demand nothing less than full control, and you will enforce that."

"These idiots hate me, Holiday. How am I going to win? You keep saying how much money we're gonna make, but I ain't never heard of some dumb sheriff making money."

Thornton brought Sheridan George into the operation because the man would shoot his own mother if he told him to. *Man doesn't have much for brains*, he thought, *but he's a good killer dog.* "Because very few of them are going to be voting, Sheridan. I want you, Iron Mike, and Jesse Cooper to be here in my office, tonight at about ten. I'll lay it all out for you. This is a good plan, so work with me."

"You're gonna have to prove it to me, Thorny, but you know I'll back you all the way. You need to worry more about Middleton than me."

"I know that, Sheridan. I know that. Now, get out of here, walk up and down the street and say hello to people. Don't take Mike with you and don't start anything else," he chuckled, watching Sheridan George scowl and walk out the door. Holiday stoked the fire, poured and drank another shot of whiskey, and went downstairs. *Thornton Town would be a good name for this place*, he thought, spotting the banker, Henry Swanson at the bar.

"Well, Henry, have you been down the street to inspect your new bank?"

Swanson stood a full six feet and a half, was fit, and dressed as befits a banker. He sipped a glass of whiskey, and drew deep on a cheroot, before answering.

"Impressive, Thornton. Do you think the brick safe is better than steel? I'm not so sure, myself."

"Well," Holiday answered, "think about it for a minute. Would you consider robbing a bank that was owned by the likes of us?" Gentle laughter was shared, and Holiday got down to business.

"How soon can you be operational? The election is next week and I'd like to get my operation under way as soon as possible."

"Wagons with outriders will be here tomorrow morning, Thornton, filled to the sideboards with money. I had to call in a lot of favors to get this, but we'll have well over two hundred fifty thousand in cash to show the railroad folk. I've promised my people full payment back, with interest within three years."

"If things go my way, we'll pay it back and have ten times that much left over for us, Henry. Good job."

"Good. I better get back. The new signs have arrived and I have a crew ready to put them up. Come by later and I'll give you a tour. Interior filled with oak, marble, slate, looks really good. We have a bank, Mr. Holiday, a bank to be proud of."

Holiday let that sink in, a wry look on his face, thinking *this is something that should be written somewhere. Thornton Holiday, building a bank, not wanted for robbing one.* He lit a big strong cigar, sipped at his whiskey and looked around his new saloon, took in the fine wood, drapery, crystal lamps hanging from long chains, and that mahogany back bar, shining its worth. *You're home, Thorny,* he thought, *for the first time in your life. Sheridan George isn't smart enough, but Swanson is. He knows what real power is, and knows I'm in control. I control my empire.*

"Did you get the mortgage forms we talked about? Can't pull this off without them. They are the heart of my plan, Henry."

"They are coming in with the money. Didn't want to have them printed up here in town," he snickered, joined by Holiday.

"I'm going to lay out some of the plan to George and the boys tonight. I don't think you need to be there. If we're seen having a drink, that's fine, but it should appear to be business, not conspiracy. Give George as much support as you think wise, in the election," Holiday said, and went back up to his office.

***

Rose Flannigan tended to Sorenson's nose and split lip, chortling just a little bit, but angry as any Irish woman could get at George and Middleton. "That was very brave, Gerald, but let's not do that again," she said, wiping away some dried blood. "Either one of those men could have shot you. You're fine now. Go into the saloon, have a bracer or two, and get back to work. I'm going down to the stockyards."

She noticed little groups of townspeople gathered as she walked down the long block to the stockyards, said good day to many, and wondered what this election would bring to the village. "Pete," she said, as she walked to one of the large corrals. "That wasn't very smart of George and Middleton. Why would someone do that just a couple of days before the election?"

"Stupidity, my dear," he said, in that deep southern drawl she enjoyed, as they walked back to the stockyard offices. "The two are nothing but troublemakers, don't give a damn about anything, and neither one can think past his own nose.

"This Holiday is up to something. If the election is honest, and I'm beginning to think that's what Holiday is up to, I would win in a landslide. But, if something happens, if the election is rigged somehow, then I won't. George acts like it's his for the taking and that's my main concern right now."

"What can we do?" Rose asked, as she slid into a chair. "How would they rig an election when everyone knows everyone else?"

Quimby handed her a tumbler partly filled with brandy, had one in his other hand, and they clinked glasses. "Just keep our eyes open, Rose. Pitts will be around all day, but he's not really a lawman. By rights, he should already have Middleton in jail for the murder of Sheriff Thomas, and should have arrested both George and Middleton for ripping up my election posters.

"He's not afraid, I'm sure. He just doesn't know what to do. Things will be different following the election. We'll clean things up good, Rose, I promise." He stood in front of the fireplace as he spoke. "Have you read my plans for the town? It took hours to get that all down on paper."

"I think it's wonderful, it's just what we need. This will be a real town, Pete, and you will be sheriff, or maybe mayor. What do you think of that?"

"Look," he said, smiling at what she said. "There's old Charlie Sloan, giving the corrals a once over." He walked to the door and called Charlie in.

"Hi, Pete. Mrs. Flannigan. Just figuring how large I should build my herd when that railroad comes in," he laughed, taking a glass of brandy from Quimby. "What's this?" he joked. "You trying to buy my vote?"

"Hope I don't have to," Quimby quipped back. "If all you boys increase your herds, I'm going to have to add more to the yards here. That's something to be happy about."

"Just walked by the new bank. I gotta say, it's impressive," Sloan said. "Last real bank I seen was in St. Loo," he drawled. "Seems a lifetime ago. Actually went into the bank," he said, "and I have to admit, it scared the hell out of me. A young swaggering cowpoke up from New Orleans, and all that marble and polished oak and money. I got out of there and ain't been in a bank since."

***

Holiday called down the bar to Jesse Cooper, "Get George, Middleton, and Colter, and come up to my office." He got the high sign from the gambler and went up the stairs, two at a time. "Now we start to bring this together," he snickered, and walked into his plush office. The others were in and seated in short order. Holiday spread glasses and a bottle around.

"Here's how we do this, gentlemen," he said, leaning against a large roll top desk across from a blazing fireplace. "These people won't know what happened, and that Quimby will be out of our hair." Holiday spent the next hour going over the plan, once, twice, three times. He was interrupted several times by George, who said that it didn't seem to make any sense.

Holiday didn't get upset or angry, and wondered why it was only Sheridan George questioning the plan. Of the group, George was far and away the smarter, yet Middleton, Cooper, and Colter never said a word. "You may not see the full benefit of what we're doing," he said, standing to signal the end of the meeting, "but you will when the money starts rolling in. Not a word to anyone about this," he said. "If I find out somebody has given us away, the death will be long and slow. Day after tomorrow, Sheridan George will be sheriff," he said, and they all agreed with big smiles.

George walked out into a gathering storm, wind coming straight out of the north, bitter cold, and he could see massive clouds building. "Should have brought one of Thorny's bottles," he muttered. "Gonna get cold tonight."

Chapter Four

E lection Day dawned with gale force, bone-freezing wind, heavy snow rumbled through the streets and between the buildings, and fires burned hot in every stove. "This will slow things down even more," Holiday joshed George. They stood near the doors of the saloon, and watched the storm. "The plan we have is excellent, Sheridan, but if we had the means, we could not have come up with anything better than this blast of winter." He was rubbing his hands in anticipation of winning the election.

"Did your men distribute those flyers?"

"Put them at every home and business except the Flannigan's, Quimby's, and Pitts's. Ranchers won't be coming in, probably, but I have men riding out to meet them if some try to get in."

"Good," Holiday said. "This storm is a godsend, really. Keep Middleton out of trouble today, don't start anything yourself, either. Let's win this election." He watched as the town slowly came to life, smoke rolled in wind driven waves from every chimney, lamps were lit, and a few stragglers braved the weather, plowing their way through knee-high drifts toward the café.

Rose Flannigan spent the night in town so she could help in the café and at the school when the polls open. Women weren't allowed to vote, but their help at the polling stations was always welcome. "The ranchers are going to have a hard time getting into town, Gerald," she said. "Better make sure we have plenty of wood stacked for the stoves."

"Been bringing in arm loads, Mrs. Flannigan," the clerk said. "Miss Sybil has the stove red hot in the kitchen. There'll be a crowd in there," he chuckled. "How many people are registered for this election?"

"Bill Pitts helped me put the list together yesterday,

and it looks like we'll have about 117 men coming through that schoolhouse today. I better get in to help Sybil and Rosie. Just listen to that wind."

***

Pete Quimby had been up for hours, fighting the storm, keeping the damage from the winds to a minimum. Fences bent and broke before the onslaught, hay stacks collapsed, winter feed scattered helter-skelter about the area, and weather stalls that couldn't stand up to the incredible force of the wind, were crushed and flung about like children's toys. *We've had winds through this area ever since I moved here, but this is the worst I can remember,* he thought, as he tried to pull the door to the office building open against the wind.

"I don't know what to do first," he chuckled, "stoke the fire or pour a glass of whiskey. Damn, I'm cold." He threw wood on the fire and poured a shot, then threw another chunk of oak in. *What a time for a storm like this. Good thing we picked the first day of spring for the election, who knows what the weather would have been like if this was still winter.*

The storm highballed down as a 'blue norther', slamming the town the previous morning, with winds getting stronger as the hours went by. The snow was right behind the winds, small cold flakes at first, then a wall of heavy, wet snow, driven by insane wind. Quimby knew it was past sunrise only because he had a clock on the desk. *It's as dark as midnight,* he thought, adding more split wood to the blazing fire.

They had set eight o'clock for the opening of the polls, and voting would continue until four that afternoon. *Hope Bill Pitts' stables can stand against this wind. He needs to be at the school to make sure that Holiday crowd doesn't become stupid. Bet most of the ranchers won't even make it to town.* Worried about his stockyard, worried about the election, and worried about the railroad coming

41

through had worn Quimby down for several weeks. "I can feel it in my bones," he said to the roaring fire, trying to get as close as possible without burning his clothes. "That bastard will try something."

He threw more wood in the great stone fireplace, poured one more shot, and headed back out the door. "I hope Sybil has the café steaming," he said, trying to walk into town. It took some doing, with winds probably in excess of fifty miles an hour, snow so thick he couldn't see ten feet, and a sheet of ice under the snow.

He noticed that he was alone on the street. "I must be the only fool in town," he laughed, barging in the café door. "Morning," he said to Sybil and Rose, trying to get out of his Mackinaw, shaking the snow and ice from his hat, and scuffing more from his boots. "Nice day to vote, eh?

"Any damage to the hotel? I've got a couple of fence lines all out of plumb, and some sheds on their way east at a high rate of speed."

"Lots of rattling around, one sign is gone, but that's about it. Gerald said he was up most of the night bringing in wood and keeping the stoves going. Today's turn-out is going to be pretty small, I'm afraid." Rose Flannigan had worry spread across her pretty face. "I know Holiday will try to foul up the process some way."

"I had a long talk with Bill Pitts yesterday, and he's going to do his best to stick right at the school house during the election. I'm hoping Holiday is smarter than to try to mess with an election.

"It does seem strangely quiet, though. Just a few of us brave souls in here for breakfast, nobody on the street. The only person I've seen this morning is that idiot Frank Colter coming out of Holiday's saloon. Fell on his butt twice," Quimby laughed. "I doubt many of the ranchers will make it in."

Small talk took up the rest of breakfast time and

Rose and Pete Quimby left for the voting booth. "Hang on to me," he laughed, trying to keep his feet under him. "I think I need more help than you."

Pitts had the fire in the big potbelly stove roaring when they arrived at the schoolhouse. "Morning, Rose, Pete. I have the voter registration book on the table for you, Rose, and I was just about to put up the flag to announce the poll's open. Last election, people were lined up already, but not today. Nice spring day like we're having, and all," he laughed, joined by the two.

"I'll help you with that flag, Bill," Pete said, pushing the door to the schoolhouse open. Thornton Holiday, Jesse Cooper, and Sheridan George were just coming up the steps. "Good morning, gentlemen," Quimby said, "We're just getting the polls open," and he held the door open for them after Pitts walked out.

"Looks like the first three votes won't be for me," Quimby snarled, holding the flagpole steady while Pitts attached the flag. "He's got quite a few votes in that new saloon of his."

"Yeah, criminal votes," Pitts said. "You have the town votes," and he tied off the lines and watched the flag doing a wild ballet at the top of the pole. "We'll need a new flag after the beating it's going to take."

***

"I can understand the ranchers not braving this horrible storm," Rose said to the group at the bar in the Red Rose Saloon, "but why didn't the town's people vote?" She, Pete Quimby, and Bill Pitts had just come from the schoolhouse after counting the votes. "One hundred seventeen men registered to vote and thirteen show up. And that horrible man Sheridan George wins by three votes.

"There's something wrong, Pete. I know it, there's something wrong."

"I'm doing everything I can to not take this personally, but there isn't any other answer I can think of.

The town didn't want to vote for me, and they shunned George too, is what I'm seeing."

"I'm seeing fraud," Rose said, "and I'm going to do something about it." She stood up as if to go somewhere, do something, knew there was nothing to do, and sat back down. "This territory has election laws and somehow election fraud owns today's vote. The governor will hear about this," she said, loud, to an all but an empty saloon.

"You can't do anything tonight, Rose. I'm going back to the stockyard, get drunk, probably, and feel sorry for myself. I'll see you in the morning," and he hunched his way into his Mackinaw and headed out into the storm.

***

"Well, Sheriff, let me be the first to buy you a congratulations drink. You'll look good wearing that star."

"I'll have to send a drawing of me wearing a sheriff's badge to the boys in Tombstone," Sheridan George said, downing a full glass of whiskey. "Quimby and that floozy of his never saw it coming," and he let out a howl of pleasure. "I think I'll lock her up in the morning for being ugly."

"We start the plan in the morning, Sheridan, so get a good night's sleep and be ready. Remember, you will need at least two fulltime deputies. Picked them?"

"Yeah," he said. "Iron Mike Middleton will be my chief deputy, and I'm gonna steal Frank Colter from you. He can get pretty mean when he wants to. Even with that arm missing, Iron Mike is fearless, and he's got a good mean streak also."

"Good," he smiled. "Enjoy yourself, Sheriff. I'll see you in the morning," and Holiday walked upstairs to his office. "I have a quick meeting with my banker," he said. "Made it through the snow, eh Swanson?" Holiday made himself comfortable in a wingback chair set near a roaring fire. "Pour a brandy and sit, we need to have a nice little talk."

44

"What do you think Quimby will do when he finds out, Thorny?"

"What can he do? He and that Flannigan woman, along with our new Sheriff, were at the polls all day. After the vote was counted, they certified it. It's a done deal, Henry, a done deal.

"Now, about these mortgage forms. I want to make sure you are completely comfortable with how they work. Never let anyone see the second copy. You understand that fully?"

"I wrote the thing, Thorny. Ease off, this will come together fine. No one in the bank but myself will ever see that second copy, and certainly, the person taking the mortgage won't. I'll give you this, though, I would never have thought up something like this. You're a genius."

"Yes, I am," Holiday beamed, wanting desperately to preen some. "I've been putting this dream together for a long time. I needed the right place, easy pickin's is how I thought of my kingdom, easy pickin's because of the small minds and stupid people. I rode into Plainsville and could feel it, knew right away that this would be the place.

"What do you think we should call it, Henry? Thorntonville? Holiday City? And I will rule this area with an iron hand. The businesses, the ranches, all mine. You'll still have your cut, Henry, don't worry about that, but this is all mine."

He drank some fire-warmed brandy and continued, "When I heard about the trouble you were having in Virginia City with the Bank of California crowd, I knew we could put this together. I've had this plan in the back of my head for years, but it needed someone like you to make it happen, and a town like this, ready to be picked clean.

"To you, sir," he said, raising the snifter and tapping Swanson's glass. "To you." The men were satisfied, shook hands and said goodnight.

Swanson had purchased a small home on the street

directly behind the new bank and fought his way there through heavy snow and howling wind, worry etched across his handsome face. *I'm going to have to get together with Sheridan George,* he thought, going over what Holiday had said. *What is Thorny thinking, kingdom, rule with iron hand, own every business and ranch? This isn't what we were putting together. I wonder if Sheridan knows all this?*

Chapter Five

"Mr. Quimby, wake up! Mr. Quimby, wake up. It's Joshua, and you have to see this, wake up!" He was more than insistent, he was shaking Pete Quimby, yelling at him, stomping his feet, anything to get the very hung-over Stockyard man awake.

"What?" Quimby finally said. "What, quit hitting, slow down, what?" and he rolled up from his bedcovers, still fully dressed, even to his muddy boots. "What are you doing, Joshua, quit," but Quimby didn't try to stand, just sat on the edge of the bed with his head in his hands. "Oh, that hurts. Did you make coffee, Josh?"

The room was spinning, his eyes wouldn't focus, and he wanted to throttle the young Pitts. All the frustration of a major storm tearing his buildings and business to shreds, and losing an election that he was sure he was going to win found their way into glass after glass of whiskey, and the consequences were unbearable.

"No, get up, you have to see this. Get up, Mr. Quimby, please," and the young man was tugging on Quimby's shirt, trying to get him to his feet. "It's on the table in the office. Come, quick. You have to see this."

It was slow, but Pete Quimby made it into his office, with help, and plopped down at his desk. Joshua handed him what looked like a flyer, a broadside, nicely printed, but wrinkled and still wet from the storm. Quimby read the poster twice, his eyes narrowing to slits of anger, his hands shaking with the desire to kill, almost ripping the paper, catching himself in time.

"Those dirty bastards," is all he could say, over and over, until he got to his feet, found his hat and jacket, and headed out the door. "Rose will kill someone, if I don't first," he growled, stomping across the stockyards toward town and the Plainsville Hotel. Joshua Pitts was right with him, step for step, plowing through heavy snowdrifts, and the remains of signs, buildings, and fences from the storm. In the few snowless patches, there was deep mud, and under the thin snow, ice.

There were at least fifteen people in the café when the two stormed in, and Rose Flannigan was already at fever pitch anger, brandishing one of the broadsides in Quimby's face. "Look at this," she screamed. "Look what those horrible men did. This is why no one came to vote. Just look," and she read from the proclamation. "Election Cancelled," she read, "by order of the New Mexico Territorial Election Commission."

Several people in the café had copies of the poster. "These were distributed all over town, Pete," she said. "To everyone except us, the Pitts's, and of course, the Holiday bandits." She sat back down, shaking with fury. "As soon as this snow and ice clear up, I'm going to Santa Fé and see the governor. This is fraud, Peter Quimby, out and out fraud.

"Well, no I know I can't go, but the governor is going to get one long detailed letter from me. Anyone else wants to sign that letter, I'll have it at the hotel desk this afternoon."

The crowd cheered, everyone saying, "Yes, I want to sign." Rose Flannigan was seething, watching as the crowd of angry people grew while the morning wore on, most trying to tell Pete how sorry they were, falling for the story. "I can't blame anyone but Thornton Holiday for this," Quimby said to the group. "This isn't your fault, in any way. This poster looks, even feels like a legal notice, so you cannot be blamed for not coming out.

"We know Holiday is not responsible for the storm, so if there had not been a storm, this may have been known as fraudulent yesterday. The damage is done; we now have to find a legal way to reverse what has happened. I don't think I'm wrong when I say there is much more behind this than simply seeing to it that Holiday has his own man as sheriff."

What that might be, he was thinking, *I can't imagine. He has a saloon, apparently is part owner of the bank, and now has his own man as sheriff. There must be a deeper plot.* He turned that over in his mind, hour after hour, even day after day.

His father was a broker for ships, moving goods from Europe and the east coast through the docks in New Orleans, so Quimby understood that fraud was often in the hearts of the human animal. When the elder Quimby began importing British and French cattle through New Orleans, destined for Missouri and Texas, Quimby was just reaching his early teens, and signed on some of the first drives into the new territory for European cattle.

Some of those people that my father had to work with were vile, he remembered as the facts of the election sank in. *Underhanded, murderous, no quarter given, and now, I'm facing the same problems my father faced. Usually there is something to be gained to make a man an outlaw, money, prestige, a woman, but I don't see any of that from what Holiday is doing.*

As the morning worked its way to noon and then afternoon, the town came to realize they had been swindled, and the anger grew. Quimby tried to keep a lid on it as much as possible, but he was frustrated by the actions of Sheriff Sheridan George and his Chief Deputy, Iron Mike Middleton.

The sheriff, with Middleton at his side, seemed to parade around town, not a smile visible from either man. They said nothing to anyone, just scowled at those they met on the sidewalks of the village. Walking side by side, swagger would be more accurate, they forced people to move aside, they purposely bumped men, intimidated women, and cursed those that stood up to them.

"It's plain enough to me," Charlie Sloan said.

"Plainsville is owned by the Holiday gang of outlaws. It's time to set aside the concept of getting help from the territory, it's time for us to stand up and fight back." Sloan was a big man, had come to the territory with his herd of Texas beef years before, squatted on a portion of a Spanish Land Grant converted to a territorial land grant, "and no bunch of outlaws is gonna push me around like this. I say, let's fight."

He discovered that the ranchers were with him all the way, but the merchants were fully intimidated, many older, many with wives and children. Sloan seethed, and found himself alone in his effort. Quimby told him that vigilante law was just as bad as what the outlaws were doing.

"Nonsense," spat Sloan. "There are enough of us on the ranches to put these beggars out." Most of those he talked with agreed with the idea, but would not participate through fear for their family or business. Even Don Jenkins a retired lawman from Texas, owner of the Plainsville Emporium worked to dissuade Sloan from forming a rancher's posse and running Holiday out of town.

***

Two men in suit coats were busy about the town distributing flyers signed by Henry Swanson, President, Plainsville Savings and Loan Bank. The bank would be open for business the following day, March 24. Bill Pitts asked one of the men about the bank. "I'm Randolph Morgan, Mr. Pitts. Mr. Swanson brought me with him from Virginia City, and I'll be chief clerk at the new bank.

"We'll be offering savings accounts, business, home, and agricultural loans and mortgages at very fair interest rates. With the railroad coming through, this little town will be an economic paradise, and the Plainsville Savings and Loan will be leading the way for all businesses."

"That's very good to hear, Mr. Morgan. I've been

wanting to enlarge my livery and blacksmith business, I may come down and talk to you about such a loan."

"I'll take care of it personally, for you Mr. Pitts. Good day," and he walked off to deliver more of his notices, visiting every home and business in the community.

People around town seemed to accept the idea of the bank; there were many conversations on the walkways, behind store counters, and at dining tables in the café. "Interesting," Quimby said to Charlie Sloan who rode in from his ranch to book some corral space for later in the spring when he would have calves for sale. "This bank is going to open just two days after Holiday fouled the community with his election fraud. That little Morgan fellow seemed like a straight arrow to me. Yet, Charlie, I know that the banker Swanson was brought here by Holiday. I'm afraid there's going to be trouble brewing in this little valley for a long time." He led Sloan out the door, walking toward the corrals and holding pens.

"Have you seen the letter that Rose Flannigan is sending to the governor? She isn't holding anything back. Already has more than one hundred signatures, and she will include a copy of the broadside that was distributed.

"No matter what you do, Charlie, don't rile her up. She'll take your head off," he laughed, as the two stood along the rail fencing in the stockyard. "That is one angry lady."

"You should be just as angry, Pete. That dirty trick was more than low, it was filthy. You should be wearing that star right now. I'm going over to the hotel and sign that letter." The two walked through the various holding pens and corrals, noting some of the damage done by the storm, and Charlie told Quimby about how many steers he would be bringing in.

"Heard any more on the train deal?" he asked as they got back to the office. "I know they can't be here this year, but with that bank opening up, I might take out a small mortgage on the ranch to build the herd for the next few years. I'm excited by the prospects, Pete. I came, with so many others from the Texas country with my herd, and I like this New Mexico range.

"What I don't like is being robbed by these great extended trail rides for the herd. I'm losing a third of my herd on those cattle drives every year." Ranchers throughout the territory were angry at how slow the railroads were in coming. One major line coming down from Colorado didn't seem to more forward more than inches a year.

"I don't know if it's those mountains the railroad men are facing, coming south out of Colorado, or a lack of desire from the territorial people, but when they finally get those rails down, they'll make money and lots of it, fast."

The Santa Fe was coming down from Colorado, there were spurs off it, but it hadn't cleared the Raton Pass yet. That road from the west though would connect with the Santa Fe when it did come further south, and the Plainsville spur would enrich this valley. Sloan, other ranchers in the area, like John Morton and Dave Peterson were set to expand their herds, and Pete Quimby was ready to expand his stockyard also.

Peterson had the largest of the area ranches, with more than fifteen cowboys working year round. His cattle ranged over thousands of acres, and one of his men also raised and trained a herd of fine horses, known for their ability to work cattle.

Quimby poured he and Charlie a steaming cup of coffee, put a little added flavor from his brandy bottle, and they settled into cane chairs. "We've answered every question that Ralph Flowers asked, even if the new sheriff is a criminal. He was elected; we do have a new bank; and there is guaranteed business for the railroad. Right now, I don't see any reason for them not wanting that spur."

"I'm going to keep an open mind on this," Sloan said. "I think after I sign that letter, I'm going to drop in on the new bank, give it a good look. You talked with Morgan, you said?"

"Yes, I did," Quimby answered, and added a bit more flavor to their mugs. "He's a friendly fellow, dresses smartly for being out in the wilds like we are, and answered every question I had. I think you will get along fine, but I got to remind you, Charlie, that bank was brought here by Holiday."

***

Crowds formed in front of the bank an hour before the scheduled opening. Morgan and Swanson had done a good job spreading the word, and when the doors opened, those still outside could hear the oohs and ahs coming from those inside. "Just look at all the marble," Rose Flannigan said to Dave Peterson when they got in the door. "And the wood. Is that teak? And the polished oak. My goodness."

Henry Swanson beamed as he stood near the entrance, inviting everyone in, while Randolph Morgan was ensconced in the cashier's cage. The two were dressed as bankers in New York City or St. Louis might be, with long dovetailed coats over immaculate shirtfronts, and silk ties. Swanson's cuffs sparkled with diamonds, his tie tack a large ruby surrounded by diamonds, and his boots shined to mirror finish.

"Looks like our bankers are well heeled," Quimby noted, joining Flannigan and Peterson. "It's interesting that Holiday, our fine sheriff, and his deputies, aren't here."

"Don't ruin my morning by talking about those scum," Flannigan said. "I hear Charlie Sloan is thinking about taking out a mortgage on his ranch to increase his herd. You gonna do the same for the yards?"

"It's sure a good thought, Rose," Quimby answered, "but I want to watch the action for a while first. How about you, Peterson?"

"Charlie and I have both been talking about it. He's pretty sure the railroad is coming, and I am too. It's a gamble, but I might just do the same as old Sloan. I can build my herd by holding back a few good heifers every year, but that would take some time. On the other hand, with a purse full of coin, I can buy a large number of good heifers, a few good bulls, and increase my herd quickly."

The tour included visits to Swanson's office complex, behind the counter of the cashier's cage, and a peek inside the great brick vault with its massive steel doors. People moved through the bank all day, Swanson finally called a halt to the tours, and closed the doors about four o'clock. "It was a good day, Mr. Morgan," he said, smiling as he took a cheroot from his vest. "I think we'll be making some loans first thing in the morning. Lock us up tight. I'm going to see Holiday at the saloon.

"Remember, when someone wants to initiate a loan, it must be done through me, only. Neither you nor any of the clerks will be making those loans or creating mortgages."

"I understand, Mr. Swanson," Morgan answered. "I'll lock up and see you in the morning. Good night."

The long walk from the bank to the Hearts of Gold Saloon allowed Swanson to pass by many of the businesses along the main street, and he tipped his hat and greeted everyone. He had a broad smile on his face meeting with Thornton Holiday at the bar.

"It was a very good opening, Thorny, just as you anticipated. There were several of the local business people and several ranchers that indicated they wanted more information on loans and mortgages. Your plan is falling into place."

"Good, Henry. I heard one problem today that only Sheridan George can handle. Seems that trollop Rose Flannigan is sending a letter to the governor about the election. I'm going to need your expert writing once again.

Here's what I want written on as close to what might look like official paper," and he handed a sheet of paper to the banker.

"I need that before noon, tomorrow. Can-do?"

"I have some blank stationery that I made up before coming down here, in anticipation of such a thing, and I'll have this for you first thing in the morning." He downed his whiskey, said goodnight and walked toward the café for his supper. Holiday told the bartender to have the sheriff come to his office as soon as he came in, and headed upstairs.

***

The weekly stage pulled up in front of the hotel at two p.m., right on schedule, with two passengers and the mail. "Hello, Rose, Gerald, it looks like spring might actually arrive. These trails are nothing but mud." The driver, Jesse Maple, threw down a mail sack, climbed down and helped his passengers out. "We'll be here two hours folks. Café is right there, and refreshments at the Red Rose Saloon. You'll hear my whistle," and he picked up the sack to take it to the post office.

"It's heavy this week, Rose. I'll drop this off, pick up the outgoing, and join you for something to eat. With the bank here," Maple said, "it looks like I'll be carrying a guard with the regular run. I'll be talking to a human instead of my horses," and he cackled long and hard, walking down the street, dragging the mail sack.

Rose and her hotel clerk went back in, he going behind the counter, she into the café. "Hello, Bill Pitts. Did I hear right that you will be adding onto your livery business?"

"I'm giving it some thought, Rose. I have room to add on, and when the railroad comes in, I think we'll see new people wanting to move here. I'm thinking of putting in a lumber mill. Joshua is already an expert at making nails and other small iron objects, and he's plenty big and strong enough to run a mill.

"I'll have to hire lumber men to cut and bring in the timber, but I'm sure there will be enough business to justify my decision." He took a long drink of water, sat back with a smile, and looked around the room. "I talked with that banker yesterday, and I think I will be able to take a mortgage on the property I have in order to get enough money to build the mill and hire the people. I'm pretty excited by the prospect."

"I'm glad for you, Bill. Make sure you know what you're signing."

Chapter Six

T he stage pulled out on time, Pete Quimby noted, watching the dust whirl around in a light wind. *We have the stage in and out, once a week,* he was thinking, *and won't it be nice when we have a railroad train coming and going once or more each week.* He walked out onto the porch of the stockyard office building, lit a cheroot, and watched Mike Middleton, Fred Colter, and Jesse Cooper ride out of town, also.

"Wonder what those fools are up to," he mumbled. "All three wearing badges, and probably all three have wanted posters up somewhere. Well, when the governor gets that letter, maybe things will change around here."

Clouds were building, promising another storm for the village, more snow piling onto the existing drifts that clogged every street, pathway, and trail. Shopkeepers were still shoveling the remains of the previous blizzard, and now faced another one.

Middleton had spent the previous two hours with Sheridan George and Thornton Holiday in the Sheriff's office. "Don't screw this up, Mike. You take Colter and Cooper with you, make sure you are not wearing those badges, cover your faces well, and get that mailbag."

"What's so damn important about a mail bag?" Iron Mike Middleton growled.

"If you don't want to work for me, Mr. Middleton," Holiday snarled, "just say so, now. You're either with me or not," and he slammed his chair, jumped to his feet, and gave every indication that he was about to shoot the man.

"OK," Middleton said. "You know I'm with you, I just don't understand what you want with a mailbag."

"I don't want the mailbag. I want you to find the package addressed to the Territorial Governor and destroy it. That's all. I don't want the driver or any of the passengers hurt in any way. Can you do this? And no rough stuff, nobody hurt."

"Yeah, I can do it. Just a letter. Why not rob the passengers, why not just shoot the driver?"

"Do it my way, Middleton," Holiday said, again, still standing and ready to pull iron. "And I better not hear otherwise. Let the stage get out an hour or so. Don't be seen following the stage out of town. There are too many eyes watching everything we do, so don't foul this up."

Middleton left the office to find Colter and Cooper. "Are you sure Middleton can be trusted to pull this off?" Holiday asked George, sitting back down at the desk. "I'm sending one of my men to Santa Fé tomorrow to mail our letter back here on next week's stage. I'll kill that fool if he screws this up."

"He's a hot head, Thorny, but he'll do fine. Henry Swanson was in earlier and dropped off a couple of names of people that have taken small loans at the bank. He said at least two of the large ranchers were interested in mortgaging their property in order in build their herds.

"It looks like your plans are coming together just like you said. At some point, I suppose, I'll understand the plan, but right now, I'm as baffled as Iron Mike. I know what is expected of me, I know I can do it. Thorny," he said, "I just don't understand why.

"The problem I see is that woman at the hotel, and Quimby. Quimby's a smart fellow and he could give us a problem. If Mike gets his blood up, that problem could be taken care of. What are we going to gain from all this? For my part, I'd just as soon walk in that bank and rob it. That's what I do best.

"And, why would you even consider owning a ranch or a bunch of dumb cows? I'll do what you say because we've always been good with each other." He paused, rubbed a grubby hand over stubble on his chin. "Quimby is the one we must get rid of if whatever it is you're working toward is going to happen."

"Quimby will have to be taken care of, George. We know that, but it's too early. We need to get things moving, on our terms, then take him and that woman out of the picture. Well," he smiled, standing up, "do your best to keep Middleton under control." He patted the sheriff on the shoulder and the two walked out of the office.

***

Middleton and company caught up with the stage and ordered the driver to stop and hand over the mail sack, which he did. "All right, now git," he yelled at the driver, firing his pistol into the air. Jesse Maple harangued his teams into a gallop wondering at the strangest stage hold-up he'd ever heard of.

When the stage pulled into Santa Fé and he told his story, few seemed willing to believe him. "The mail sack?" most asked, not understanding. Maple said the three men, all wearing bandannas over their faces, one of them having just one arm, robbed him of just the mail sack. "Didn't even look at the passengers," he said.

The Santa Fé police were quick to alert federal marshals of the robbery, by telegraph. The marshal was in Texas on other business and would get back to New Mexico Territory as soon as possible. Since no one was hurt, no money stolen or missing, the Santa Fé police did not put a high priority on the matter.

When Holiday's man reached the territorial capitol, the story was still being discussed. "Boss will be glad to know that Iron Mike pulled it off nice and neat." He put the fake letter in the mail system and it would be delivered on the next stage through Plainsville, as if in answer from the governor.

***

Over the next week, the bank was the center of activity. Businesses opened regular accounts, several people took out personal loans, a few took out property mortgages, among them, John Morton on his large cattle ranch north of town. "I have excellent grass, Mr. Swanson," he said, "and have the deed to two sections of good prairie. Right now, I'm only running about sixty cows and five bulls and I would like to expand that herd."

"I know your land, John," Henry Swanson said. "I've been there. I would be able to offer you a substantial loan if you mortgaged the property. How much were you thinking of?"

"I'd like to start with at least another hundred and fifty heifers, and enough bulls to cover them, and add some equipment so I can grow grass and grain to mow for winter feeding. I think two thousand dollars should handle that."

"If you think that's enough. With your ranching background and property you have, I would be willing to go as high as five thousand if you need it." He had a grand smile on his face as he reached into a drawer and pulled some papers out. "Just name your figure."

Morton settled on twenty five hundred dollars and Swanson filled out the papers. "Now, just sign here," he said, putting the top sheet in front of Morton, then, laying it over the second sheet, but leaving the signature line open, "and here."

John Morton glanced at the sheet, signed it, dipped the pen, and signed the line on the second sheet. "That's fine, John, just fine. Let's go visit with Mr. Morgan and get your line of credit set up. You make your deals with the stock people and they can draw the money from your credit line."

"Thank you, Mr. Swanson. When that railroad comes through, I'll have several hundred head of fine, well-fed beef to ship."

The two bankers watched Morton walk out of the bank, his copy of the mortgage safely tucked in his coat pocket. He had a wide smile on his face, and headed straight for the Red Rose Saloon. "That's the first one, Morgan," Swanson said. "He'll tell his rancher friends how easy the process is, and we should have them lined up into the street." He chomped on his cigar for a couple of minutes, stood in the sun on the bank's porch, smiling at those walking by, and slipped back inside to finish up the day.

Morgan met Charlie Sloan and Bill Pitts at the bar. "Well, I did it," he exclaimed, and signaled Old Pete for a beer. "Swanson wasn't kidding about how easy it is to borrow enough to make the improvements I need. I now have a credit line of twenty five hundred big old dollars at that bank.

"Here's the letter of introduction I will need when I get to Santa Fé and buy those heifers. If I use my own men, I can bring them back here in one bunch and not have to hire those trail thieves."

"I'm glad for you, John," Sloan said. "Let's see what the loan paper looks like." Morton handed the sheet of paper to him and he read for a couple of minutes. "Well, this is simple enough; looks like a fair interest rate and plenty of time to pay it off. Listening to you and reading this has just about made up my mind. I think I'll head back to the ranch and do some serious planning. See you boys," he said, his glass emptied and he headed out the door.

Pitts and Morton had another drink and Pitts, too left for the livery stable. "Josh," he hollered, walking into the blacksmith area of the large complex. "Come here, boy, we need to talk."

"What is it, Pa?" he asked, running in. "What's the matter?"

"Ain't nothing wrong, boy. Fetch me a cup of coffee and get something for yourself. We have some planning to do. We're going into the lumber business, I think, and it's going to take the two of us to pull it off. You're about to be the man you already think you are, son," he smiled, put a couple of chairs next to a beat up old table, and wiped it clean with his shirt sleeve.

The bank remained busy as the town and outlying farms and ranches became aware of how easy getting a loan or mortgage was. Pitts took out a mortgage on the livery and blacksmith business, Dave Peterson, one on his ranch for herd improvement, one from Quimby for improvements to the stockyards, and one from Charlie Sloan on his ranch. Rose Flannigan gave the idea some thought, and talked about it as she and Doc Winters had breakfast one morning.

"This old hotel could use some maintenance, Doc," she said, watching him peck at a couple of fried eggs. "Windows are loose, beds are old, need new bedding. Business has been good, but a loan would make these projects a lot easier."

"I don't believe in credit at all," Doc Winters said. "People think it's free money. Well, it ain't. Nothin's free, Rose. You end up beholden to someone and then you pay high interest for the right to be in debt. No, Sir, I pay for something or I don't get it."

"That's always been my way too, Doc," she said, "but having that bank here, and willing to help out the businesses and the ranchers, well, it's sure a friendly temptation." She got up to get them more coffee just as Pete Quimby came in.

"Mind if I join you?" he said, sliding into an empty chair. "I'm one hungry cowboy this morning. Doc, how you holding up?"

"I'm fine, Pete, just fine. We're talking about the bank and all the loans that are being made. Are you satisfied with what you signed?"

"I am," Pete said, as Rose sat back down. "The interest rate is very fair, and length of the loan is fine with me, and the only question I have concerns the railroad, not the bank. If that road isn't pushed through, I'm going to have the largest, emptiest stockyard in New Mexico Territory." He wasn't smiling at that last comment.

Doc Winters said, "You worry about that railroad,

Pete, I'm far more worried about Holiday and his bunch. Sheriff George is a mean person and that Mike Middleton has evil in his heart. When I was a kid, Middleton would have been known as a bully. Hell, he is a bully."

"Well now, Doc, you've found a soapbox to stand on," Quimby joshed. "I think you're right, though. Some way that bank is tied to whatever criminal activity Holiday is planning, but for the life of me, I can't figure it out."

Rose Flannigan sat back listening to the men. "I think we need to create some sort of defense for us," she said, as she wiped away crumbs of toast. "We call Plainsville a town, but it isn't really. We don't have a town board; we don't have any laws or rules other than those of New Mexico Territory. We don't pay any town taxes," and smiled as she said it. "We think we're in some county called Torrez, but is that real? I don't think so."

She looked around the table, took in the entire room, and continued. "Sometimes I think that Charlie Sloan has the right answer. Form a vigilante group and run the fools out of the area." She paused, smiled gently, and said, "then I think of the families, of the children, and I know that's wrong. We need to build a real town."

Both men liked the idea and for the next two hours, as they consumed large pots of steaming coffee, the three laid out plans to create the town of Plainsville. At the end, they funded the printing of broadsides to be distributed to every business, family, and individual in the area. It called for a meeting to create the township, called for an election to town boards to create the laws under which the population would live.

"And, don't forget, all this has to be paid for," Rose said, "so there will have to be plans for taxes, on properties and businesses.

"If you remember, Pete, this was your idea. You brought this to me and I've been working on it ever since." Flannigan smiled at the big man.

"This is a giant step forward," Doc Winters said, standing and stretching after the long time at the table. "What do you think the railroad people with think?"

"I think it's exactly what Ralph Flowers was asking for," Quimby said. "I'm worried now about what Holiday might do. By the way, Rose, isn't that stage due today, or am I off schedule again?"

"Should be here about two," she said.

Chapter Seven

Holiday and Sheriff George were just outside the Hearts of Gold Saloon when Jesse Maple drove the stage into town. "This is going to be more than interesting when they get that letter from Santa Fé," Holiday said. "I think today would be a good day to initiate step two in our plan. Get with your deputy Colter and Jesse Cooper, and work something out."

"I'll make the rounds, see who's in town, and get things started."

"Remember, they cannot live. They cannot be allowed to say anything to anyone."

"I understand, Thorny, I'll do it just the way we planned. Go have a drink, relax," and Sheridan George was actually smiling as he walked off the porch toward town. Holiday slipped back into the saloon and went straight to his office. *I wish I could figure out just what this grand master plan is*, the sheriff thought, walking back toward his office. *Robbing banks has always been his game, now he builds one. And I'm the sheriff?*

People moved out of the way as George walked down the boardwalk, many had the same thoughts as the sheriff. "What's he doing as sheriff?" Don Jenkins owned the Plainsville Emporium, had arrived several years ago, coming further west from Texas. He was older than most in the frontier village, retiring from a long career in law-enforcement. Pete Quimby had approached him to run for sheriff before taking on the task himself, but Jenkins had said no, thanks.

Jenkins watched the sheriff strut down the street, not giving an inch to those coming toward him, not smiling, not saying howdy or even go to hell. "Typical outlaw," Jenkins muttered, standing in the doorway of his store. He was thinking of his first few years as a Texas deputy sheriff, deputy marshal for a while, and sheriff more than once. One old law dog explained the facts of life this way. "Someday you're gonna need some help, some back-up, and all those people you pissed on are gonna turn their backs. You help people, you be nice to those that obey the law, and they'll remember." Jenkins knew that the only friends Sheriff George had were other outlaws.

"Whatever Holiday and that bunch are up to, I hope they stay away from me," Jenkins commented, stepping back into his shop. "Damn shame what they did to Pete."

Maple had the mailbag down on the ground and was helping the passengers out of the stage as George walked up. "Heard you had a little problem last time through, Maple. Everything go right this trip?"

"Sure did, Sheriff, yes sir. Now, that robbery was the strangest I ever heard of," and he grabbed the sack, threw it over his shoulder and headed for the post office. George continued down the street, still wearing a smile.

"Wonder what the sheriff meant by that?" hotel clerk Gerald Sorenson muttered, escorting the stage passengers toward the restaurant for their meal. Sorenson pondered the thought for a few minutes, and went back to work behind the hotel desk.

***

Pete Quimby was covered in dirt and grime from repairing some of his buildings and equipment, doing cleanup work around the stockyard, and wanted something cold and strong as he strode toward his office. He watched Rose Flannigan all but running toward him, flashing a piece of paper in the air. "Pete. Pete," she called, getting closer "Look at this." She stopped before running the man down. "The letter from the governor," she was panting so hard the words were all choked together. "The governor," she said, and Quimby took the letter from her as they walked into his office.

"Sit down," he said. "Let me get us a drink. Catch your breath, Rose, what on earth," And he poured some whiskey in two cups and sat down to read the letter. "This isn't right," he said, and read the letter out loud, maybe to better understand it.

"To the citizens of Plainsville, New Mexico Territory

"Greetings; Please be advised that the only elections this office has any control over are those involving territory-wide offices. Since what you described is a local election, we have no jurisdiction, therefore are unable to assist in any local problems that may have been encountered.

"Local elections are at the discretion of local authorities and if there were improprieties involved, it would be the responsibility of local authorities to take whatever action might be necessary.

"Kindest regards, Nelson T. Thackeray, Territorial Secretary"

Quimby sat back in his cane chair, took a healthy drink of whiskey, and looked at Rose Flannigan, then the letter, then the floor, and finally, back to Rose. "There's something wrong, Rose, but I haven't got it yet." He read the short letter again, saying, "Your letter with about one hundred signatures was sent to the governor. I've sent letters to the governor before, particularly recently, dealing with the constant cattle rustling, and working to get the railroad spur into Plainsville.

"He has always responded by saying something to the effect, 'I received your note and passed it on to whoever, and they responded this way.' This secretary didn't say, in response to your letter, the governor asked me to answer your questions. That's what I would have expected from this governor. This letter is a fake.

"And of course, another problem, how the hell do we prove that?" Morose would be a good way to describe the atmosphere in the stockyard office. "Anything else come on that stage to make today a complete disaster?"

Rose Flannigan choked on a chuckle, saying, "Just a couple of passengers heading to Taos. I better get back and make sure Jesse Maple gets everybody on board. Come by later and we can have a drink before supper." She hurried up the street, the letter clutched tightly, seeing Maple already getting his passengers on board, hoisting the mailbag up to the seat.

"Well, Rose, I'm off. See you next month."

"Have a safe trip, Jesse," she said, stepping onto the boardwalk in front of the hotel. Maple called to his four-up and moved the stage briskly toward the Santa Fé Road, the leaders prancing a little bit and the wheelers doing the heavy work. "That's a beautiful sight, isn't it?" she said to Gerald Sorenson standing at the open doors of the hotel. "Wait 'till that railroad starts making its runs," she smiled, walking into the large building.

"Did you know what Maple meant about a robbery on his last run?" Sorenson asked as they walked across the lobby.

"Robbery?" Rose asked. "I haven't heard of any robbery. What did he say?"

"He was talking to the sheriff. He said it was the strangest robbery he had ever heard of. All the bandits wanted was the mailbag." Flannigan stopped dead in her tracks and spun on the small clerk.

"The mailbag?" she barked. "Someone stole the mailbag from the stage last month? Is that what you just said?" Rose Flannigan's eyes blazed and the Irish fury was not contained. "Those bastards," she belted out loud enough to have been heard on the street. "Quimby was right," she said, a little calmer as she stormed out of the hotel, and marched back across town to the stockyards, muttering with each step, "Those bastards."

***

"John Morton's in town, Thorny," George said, meeting the saloonkeeper on the street. "We'll work it out fine. As it comes down, you stay out of it, no matter what seems to be taking place. In fact, it's best if you just stay in your office this evening."

"You're right, Sheridan. I don't want to be involved in any way or even be seen with whatever you have planned. And, don't tell me. Wait until after. I'll figure it out." They said goodbye, George walked toward his office and Holiday ambled down the street toward his saloon. "I guess I won't get to say so-long to Mr. Morton," he muttered.

George found Iron Mike Middleton and Frank Colter in the office, poured a glass of whiskey from a flask on the table, and sat down. "I'm only going to say this once, gentlemen, so listen closely and don't give me any arguments. Both of you know the rancher John Morton," and the two nodded their heads. "He's having drinks at the Hearts of Gold Saloon and Slim is feeding him strong liquor. Morton isn't a good drinker in the first place and this stuff will knock him a good one." All three men chuckled, and George continued. "Morton is quick tempered and Conrad is going to pick a fight with him. He'll either be shot dead or if he should get lucky and get away, we will chase him and see to it that he is shot dead.

"Any questions?"

"What do we do?" Middleton asked, "Just hang around and wait?"

"Yup," George said. "Have your horses saddled and ready, and if Morton does run from the saloon, let him get far enough out of town so nobody can see. Shoot him dead. Do not bring a live Mr. Morton back to town." He poured another glass of whiskey, lit a cheroot, and sat back in his chair.

"Take your horses down near the livery and just wait. You may not have to go anywhere, but be ready."

Middleton and Colter walked out of the office and walked their mounts down the street. "Do you understand what this is all about?" Middleton asked, shaking his head. "Why not just walk in and shoot the bastard?"

"We're wearing badges, Mike. Holiday and George want Morton dead but it has to appear as a legal death. Deputy sheriffs don't just walk in and shoot someone." He wanted to laugh at Iron Mike but figured he'd probably get shot if he did.

They tethered their horses near the livery and stood in the shadows of a tree, keeping a close eye on the front of the saloon, listening to the music. Both wanted to be inside drinking.

"That railroad's gonna make me a rich man," John Morton said, feeling the effects of some pretty strong whiskey. "My herd's gonna be one of the biggest in the territory."

"What do you know about railroads, anyway," Thomas Conrad snarled. "A real rancher would be at his ranch, not getting' all liquored up and prideful."

"You got no right to talk like that," Morton said, his face flushed from anger and liquor. He flexed his hands into fists and rocked back on his heels. He stood almost six feet tall and was just as strong as he was large. Forty years old, all but two of those on ranches in Texas and New Mexico have made him big and tough, and his temper equally quick and mean. "I don't like people talking to me like that."

"Then do somethin' about it, cowboy," Conrad jibed as he turned to face Morton, less than eight feet separating the two. Conrad had the stub of a cheroot in his mouth, tobacco juice stained the stubble of a beard, and the thrill of a fight spread across an ugly face. He took a step toward Morton, as if to swing on him when Morton jerked his revolver before Conrad could and fired once, twice, three times, driving the once feared gunman back at least fifteen feet.

Conrad lay on his back with three big holes in his

chest, his shirt and coat splashed with blood, his eyes glazed, staring at the ceiling. Morton stood quiet for just a moment, realized through the fog of booze what he had done, spun and ran for the door. No one gave chase.

His horse was tied in front of the saloon, and he released the quick knot, jumped into the saddle, and rode out of Plainsville at a full gallop. Within seconds, two men followed him out of town. One of the gamblers went upstairs to Holiday's office to find the boss and tell him what had happened.

***

Old Pete poured whiskey for Pete Quimby and Rose Flannigan, and moved back down the bar, talking to himself. "Stay away from them two tonight," he muttered, wiping the bar as he walked. "When they be fire in her eyes like that, somebody's gonna get hurt."

"Gunshots," somebody yelled from near the big doors. "Sounds like coming from the Hearts of Gold," he said, from the boardwalk. Quimby, Rose, and most of the patrons followed, and were able to see somebody on a horse as it raced out of town, the two deputies not far behind.

"Couldn't tell who that was," Quimby said. "Looks like Iron Mike and Colter will try to run him down."

Sheriff Sheridan George walked from his office, almost casually, Quimby thought, toward Holiday's saloon. "Evening, folks," he said, as he all but strolled by the Red Rose and the group on the boardwalk. "Sounded like a shooting." As he continued, Pete Quimby and a few others followed a few steps behind.

"Old Tom Conrad picked a fight with the wrong man," the bartender said, as George stood over the body.

"I don't see it that way," Holiday said. "That rancher John Morton came in here just itching for a fight all night, was nickin' on Conrad, pressin' the point, daring Conrad to fight. Morton, out of nowhere, just drew his

71

weapon and shot poor old Tom three times. Look, Sheriff," Holiday continued, "Conrad's gun is still in the holster. This was murder, sure as I'm standing here."

No one in the saloon mentioned that Holiday was not on the saloon floor when the fracas took place; everyone just nodded approval at what the boss said. "Well, sure looks that way to me," Sheriff George said. "Let's get this mess cleaned up. You say it was Morton did this? The rancher Morton?"

The bartender and half the crowd said yes, it was John Morton, and George continued. "Well, then, let's get up a posse and ride out to the Morton ranch. Anyone want to ride with me?" he asked, and half a dozen men jumped at the chance. "If we bring him in, there's two dollars for each of you, and if we can't, I'll buy a round for you," and they hustled out to find and saddle horses for the ride.

"You're not going?" Rose asked Pete Quimby when he came back to the Red Rose.

"No, I don't think so," he smiled. "I'd shoot the sheriff or he'd shoot me." He stood quiet for a short time, then said, "I can't picture John Morton picking a fight with a known gunman, then shooting him in cold blood. There's no doubt, though, I guess. I saw Conrad's body, three shots to the chest, and Conrad did not draw his gun. Just doesn't sound like John," he said again.

Two hours later the posse, led by the sheriff and his two deputies came back to town, leading a horse that cradled a body draped across the saddle. "We caught up with the murderin' bastard about two miles out of town," Middleton bragged as they rode through town, toward the sheriff's office, followed by patrons from both saloons. "He tried to put up a fight, took a shot at old Colter there, but I shot him dead. He won't be killin' nobody again," and he puffed himself up some, as he stepped off his lathered horse.

"Here you go boys, just like I promised," the sheriff

said, handing out two-dollar coins to the six men that rode in the posse. "Now, don't spend them all at once," he joked to laughter from many in the crowd. "I won't tolerate this kind of stuff in Plainsville. Those that want to rob and hurt and murder will have to find other towns and places to do their dirty work. As sheriff, I will see to it that Plainsville is a safe place to live and raise a family."

"Don't choke," Rose said, as Quimby coughed lightly at George's little speech.

"The biggest criminal in town talking about keeping the peace. I'm not choking, Rose, I'm about to throw up."

Chapter Eight

"**B**efore we talk about John Morton and his apparent killing of Tom Conrad, I want to talk about our letter to the governor." Pete Quimby said to Rose Flannigan, Dave Peterson, Peterson's ranch manager Reynaldo Cortez, Bill Pitts and a couple of others at the stockyard. He had a large pot of coffee boiling on the stove and ample whiskey to flavor it on a brisk early spring morning.

"Our little town of Plainsville is being taken over by outlaws of every kind, not just gunslingers and gamblers, these men are taking over the town, every business, every ranch, every possible opportunity to rob and steal from all of us. We sent a letter to the governor last month and got a response to that letter just two days ago. The response, my friends, did not come from the governor."

The men looked at Quimby, then to Rose, heads twisted, murmurs and muttering were offered up, and Quimby continued. "It seems that Jesse Maple was the victim of a robbery after he left town a few weeks ago, and according to him, the only thing stolen was the mail sack."

"How do you know that?" Bill Pitts asked. "The sheriff hasn't said anything, that I've heard."

"Jesse told Gerald Sorenson about the robbery. He reported it to his superiors and the sheriff in Santa Fé. What that means," Quimby continued, "is simple. The governor never received our letter."

Dave Peterson just shook his head, squirmed around in his chair, and finally piped up. "If he didn't get the letter, how the hell did he respond?" There were snickers, which led Peterson to shoot ugly scowls around the room. "Maybe I don't think as fast as some of you," he growled, "but that's really strange to me."

"That's the point, Dave," Rose Flannigan said. "He didn't get the letter and it wasn't the governor that

74

responded. Holiday had some of his men rob the stage, and a return letter already in Santa Fé, ready to send back to us."

"That's the way I see it," Quimby said. "The entire election was a fraud from the start, and no one in Santa Fé is aware of that." He poured another cup of coffee, with a bit of sweetener, which gave those in the room time to take in the situation. "All of us here have an economic interest in Plainsville, whether it be a business or a ranch, and all of us are supporters of the railroad coming through town.

"We have very little time, I'm afraid in which to clean up this mess. And, I'm afraid the mess just got more ugly. The John Morton murder is far more than what we have been told. Before I get into that, I'd like to hear some comments on how we can end this siege by the Holiday gang."

Bill Pitts stood up and stretched, poured some coffee, went to the window facing the dusty main street. "I know what I would like," he said, walking slowly back to his chair, but not sitting. "I'd like to make this a real town, with rules and laws, with an elected town council," and he took a long pause, gulped some coffee, paced around a bit, finally took his seat. He slowly continued, "But I don't know how we would do that."

"That's exactly what the railroad wants, also," Quimby said. "We can't just call for an election, as we did for sheriff. These people are ahead of us on that issue. But, I think I know a way that will work." His turn to stand up, and he paced about the room, sipped some coffee, poured more, and sat back down.

"We have neglected our most important means of communication, and our local gangster, Thornton Holiday hasn't. We sent our letter to the governor by mail on the stagecoach while all the time, right in the middle of town, connected by a swinging door, is the telegraph office.

"Rose, do you have a copy of the letter we sent?"

"I do, but of course, not with all the names signed, as the original had."

"Don't make a big deal of this, but simply take that letter and send it by telegraph to the governor. Make me a copy, and I'm leaving this afternoon for Santa Fé, without any fanfare. Nobody say a word, and I'll make it. If Holiday finds out, he'll have me murdered out on the trail by one of George's deputies.

"I can be in Santa Fé in two days, meet with the territorial governor, get the necessary information on forming a legal township, and be back before Holiday knows I've gone off. If anyone asks where I am, simply say you don't know."

"Want someone to ride with you?" Bill Pitts asked.

"No. It's best if I go alone."

Peterson got up and walked around some, shaking his head. "I wonder what got into old John Morton to get in a gun fight with Conrad?"

"They filled him with whiskey, and you know John's temper," Quimby said, "and then Conrad just prodded until Morton responded. What I don't understand, I got the impression at the time that everything was preplanned. Middleton and Colter were with their horses ready to chase, the sheriff casually asked for a posse." Quimby walked around the room some more, there was chatter from the group, but nobody had any answers.

"I think Sloan is right," Peterson finally said. "We need to bring our men into town and run these fools out. That's the only answer." He shook his head again. "I know I'm not a gunslinger, but I also know I have five or six really good cowboys working for me, Sloan has more, and Morton's men would join, I'm sure."

"I could bring four men with me this afternoon," Reynaldo Cortez said, "if you say the word, Dave."

"Vigilante law isn't the answer," Pete Quimby said again, with enough emphasis that those in the room accepted his statement as fact. "I'll leave for Santa Fé right away, and we'll do this according to the law." There were grumbles from Sloan and Peterson, but everyone agreed that Pete should ride to the capitol as fast as possible.

The meeting broke up with most heading to the Red Rose Saloon. Rose walked back to the hotel with Cortez, to get the letter copied for Pete. "I don't want any more killing, Reynaldo," she said to the lanky ranch manager, "but sometimes I think Charlie Sloan is right about just attacking the Holiday gang."

"Many people would die, Rose," he said, "and many innocent people would be hurt, I'm afraid. I could put together enough men to roust those fools out, but I really don't want to." She stopped while he was talking and just looked at him.

"I don't want anyone else to get hurt, Rey." She smiled at him, not coyly, but directly, her brilliant green eyes sparkling. "Especially you. Are you going to stay in town for a while, today. Maybe we could have supper together."

"I can't Rose, I promised Dave I'd move some cattle this afternoon, and we have miles of ditch that needs cleaning after that storm. I'll be in town as soon as that work is taken care of. Dave wants me to book some space with Pete for a shipment later this spring.

"I miss spending time with you. We'll make up for that soon," and he squeezed her hand, giving her a big smile, stepped into the saddle and rode out of town, toward the Peterson ranch.

Rose watched until the trail took him out of sight and walked into the hotel to find the governor's letter. She took her copy to the telegraph office, then headed to the stockyards. "Be careful, Pete," she said, as she handed him his copy. "Those men are murderers, as you already know. Remember me to Governor Monahan. He and my late husband were friends many years ago, when he was a judge in Missouri.

"After you're hours out of town, I'll send another telegram to him, saying you are coming on urgent business."

"No, Rose. Wait at least until sometime tomorrow to send that. I need to have lots of distance between me and this town."

They said goodbye, and Rose walked slowly back to the hotel, thoughts of the governor responding to the town's situation, thoughts of having a real relationship with Reynaldo Cortez, and thoughts of Quimby making the long ride to the capitol safely. *There are times I envy these men. They talk about putting together a force and wiping out a gang like Holiday's. I could do that, but then they would remind me that women don't do that. Well, I could.* She was marching with anger by the time she reached the hotel. Even Gerald Sorenson seemed afraid to say anything when she walked to her office.

Quimby put a quick pack together for his long, fast ride to the Territorial Capitol, walked into the stables at the stockyard and saddled up one of his best horses. "I'm still thinking I should take a pack animal," he thought, adjusting his bedroll and pack to the back of the saddle. "Just slow me down, and I have to be quick on this ride." He didn't ride straight for the Santa Fé road, instead he headed out toward Charlie Sloan's ranch, cut cross-country to the main road, and put his strong thoroughbred into a long trot.

Frank Colter sat on the bench outside the Sheriff's Office and watched as Quimby rode out of town. He didn't mention that to Sheridan George until much later that evening.

"You saw that fool ride out of town with a pack on the back of his saddle and didn't say anything? Damn you, Colter." George was ready to shoot his deputy on the spot. "Middleton," he howled at the big man passed out from an afternoon of drinking. "Get your butt in here.

"You and Colter ride out. Follow the trail that Quimby left, and find him. Make sure he puts up a fight before you kill him. No questions, git." He was ready to shoot both men.

***

The next morning, Rose Flannigan finished breakfast in the café and walked toward the telegraph office to send a wire to the governor. As she neared the bank, she ran into Henry Swanson, getting the doors open for business. "Good morning, Mrs. Flannigan," he said. "Looks like spring has finally arrived in our fair city."

"Good morning, Mr. Swanson," she answered, coolly. "By the way," she said, stopping in front of the man. "Do you know whether John Morton left a will? And, what will happen to his ranch now that he is deceased?"

"As to a will, I'm not aware of one. He took out a mortgage on his property, as you know, and one of the points in our contract with him states that if he should die before the mortgage is paid off, the property reverts to the bank. I will be filing those papers with the Territory this week."

"Is that a normal clause in a bank mortgage?" she asked, stunned by the statement. "I've never heard of such a thing."

"That's what Mr. Morton asked for, since there are no known relatives that might lay claim to the property. I'll be happy to show you the mortgage he signed, if you feel there's something amiss," he said, smiling, tipping his hat, and stepping back into the bank.

"That won't be necessary," Rose said, taking the few steps toward the telegraph office. She sent the note to the governor, and walked back to the hotel, a grim look on her normally open Irish face.

"Is that anger or contemplation I see," Bill Pitts said, as she sat down at a table in the café. "Pete Quimby won't be back for several days. He wanted to place an order for some lumber for the building he's planning. That mill will be set up by this time next week, and I'm getting logs in already."

"That's good, Bill," she said. "Have you got a couple of minutes you can spare? We need to have a nice little chat in my office."

"Sure Rose. Is something wrong?" She walked over to the kitchen and poured each of them large mugs of coffee, and led the way back to her office.

Pitts settled his large frame into a small wooden office chair as Rose set the coffee down and took her seat behind a petite desk that would barely hold a sheet of paper, pens, and ink. She looked a long time into the eyes of Bill Pitts before speaking.

"Pete should be in Santa Fé by this time tomorrow, Bill. But that isn't what I need to talk to you about."

"I should have ridden with him. I tried to tell him that but he wouldn't listen. My God, what happens if the Holiday bunch finds out? He can't hold off the entire George gang."

"He'll be fine, Bill. Quimby's a big man, fine shot, and good horseman. I saw him leave on that big thoroughbred of his, so he'll make good time getting there. There's another reason I want to talk with you." She sat back in her chair, took a long drink of now almost cold coffee, and told Pitts what she learned from the banker about John Morton's mortgage. "Did you have the same clause written into your loan?" she asked.

"No, not at all," he said, getting to his feet. "That is unusual, to say the least. I've had mortgages before, back east before Joshua and I moved to the territory. If I should die before the mortgage is paid off, the property transfers to Joshua and he then becomes responsible for the loan.

"I've never heard of such a thing," he said again, pacing around the small office space. "Did that banker show you the paperwork?"

80

"No, but he did offer to show me, so it must be true. Can you take a good look at your paperwork, just to be sure? I don't trust Swanson any more than I trust Holiday, and this really worries me."

"I'll go get it right now. Did you take out a mortgage? I know you were thinking of it. I know that Pete did, and so did Charlie Sloan. I think that Dave Peterson did as well." He stood up, grim faced and angry, fists balled tight. "Has anyone seen the copy of the contract that Morton should have held?"

Flannigan indicated she didn't know, and Pitts continued, "I'll be back within the hour, Rose, and we can at least be sure of mine."

On his way back to the livery and blacksmith shop, Pitts noticed Mike Middleton and Frank Colter ride into town on worn out horses. "Those two should be whipped," he muttered, looking at the condition of the animals. "Treating fine animals like that makes me angry enough to do something," he continued, as he strode to the livery.

Middleton and Colter tied their horses in front of the office and walked in. "Well?" George demanded immediately. "Is that bastard dead? I don't see no body out there."

"Couldn't catch him," Middleton said, as he slumped into a chair. "Saw what we figured was his dust once, miles in front of us. Never really saw him."

"So, you just gave up? What the hell kind of men are you?" he roared, slamming his ham of a fist onto the wall, which shook the whole building. "Send little boys out to do a man's work," he spat tobacco juice onto Middleton's boots.

Iron Mike jumped to his feet, reaching for his gun, finding the big open barrel of a large caliber revolver about to be shoved up his nose. "Sit down," George snarled, "before I splash your empty head all over this office. I told you to run him down, kill that bastard, and bring the body back to town. And you gave up. Holiday will love this," he said, and slammed that fist into the wall again. He slowly uncocked the revolver and put it in its holster, sneered at the two men, who in turn were looking like hangdog children being reprimanded.

George slammed out of the office, and marched toward the Hearts of Gold Saloon, daring anyone in his path to say something, or even look at him. Middleton found his courage after George left the office.

"If he ever talks to me like that again, I'll shoot him dead." Colter didn't say a word, just walked out the door, headed for the saloon as well. Neither man bothered to take care of their horses.

"All the men you could have brought in for this job, Holiday, and you had to bring Middleton." Sheridan George steamed, slammed his glass to the bar, daring the bartender to say something. "We lost Quimby. He's on his way to Santa Fé and there isn't anything we can do about it."

"My turn to calm you down, George. Take it easy. Let's move on a couple of property owners today, maybe old man Jenkins at the Emporium, and that fool Dave Peterson. Then, tomorrow, let's initiate the new Law Enforcement Tax we talked about. I have the posters ready to distribute.

"Go back, get Middleton under control, don't shoot him, and let's keep this program moving forward. We'll deal with Quimby when he gets back. After all, George, there isn't one single thing the governor can do. This is our town now, we make the rules." He took a long drag on his cheroot, downed half a glass of whiskey, patted the sheriff on the shoulder, and strolled up the stairs, shoulders back and head high. After all, that would be the royal way.

Yes sir, he said to himself, *this is our town now, and we make the rules. I think I'll take that Plainsville Hotel building and turn it into the Thornton Holiday Memorial*

Town Hall. Maybe even have a statue made to sit in front.
Holiday's eyes were slightly glazed as he reached the top of
the stairs and made his way to his office. No one heard, but
there was chuckling as he walked in.

George had one more drink, calmed himself down
and headed back to his office. "All right, you two, you get
one more chance, then I'll let Holiday figure out what to do
with you. That's one angry man right now, letting Quimby
just ride out of town, but we have work to do.

"Old man Jenkins, Don Jenkins, at the Plainsville
Emporium took out a mortgage on the business. He's a
former Texas Ranger, so when you provoke him remember
that. He's probably faster and better than either of you, but
there are two of you. Make damn sure the man is dead, no
questions.

"Now get out of my sight before I shoot you," he
snarled, and Middleton and Colter left in a hurry, walking
straight across the street to the Emporium as it's normally
called. The sign, hung proudly in front of the store read,
Plainsville Emporium Dry Goods, Feed, Implements,
Equipment. Jenkins, almost sixty and retired from a long
life as a lawman in Texas, Missouri, and service as an
artillery officer with the Confederate Army during the war,
settled in Plainsville several years ago. He wears his
revolver in an old Confederate Army holster still.

Never married, he has been Grandfather to every
kid in the area, gave sleigh rides and wagon rides to hordes
of children at every opportunity, and probably could end up
as mayor of the town, once all these problems are solved.
"Well, this is a surprise," he said. "Deputies, welcome to
the Emporium. What can I do for you? Got some new Colts
you might be interested in." His smile was warm and he
walked around the counter to wait on Middleton and Colter.

Middleton stood near the door and Colter walked
toward the back of the store, which put Jenkins at an angle
between them. "We got a lot of complaints against you,

Jenkins. You been cheatin' people all over town. Sheriff says we have to close your business and arrest you. Put your hands on the counter where I can see them.

"Colter. Go round behind the counter and relieve this ugly varmint of his weapon. You come peace-able, Jenkins."

Jenkins was faster than Middleton had ever seen, and the storekeeper spun around, his big Colt put two rounds through Colter's heart, and as he turned to gun down Middleton, took a shot between the eyes from the one-armed deputy. As he fell, Jenkins' gun went off a third time; a bullet tore through Middleton's leg, knocking him to the floor.

People in the bank, post office, hotel and saloon, along with Sheriff George ran as a herd to the store following all the gunfire. "Keep back folks," George growled at those arriving. "Middleton," he yelled as he pushed through the door. He found his chief deputy bleeding from his thigh, then saw Colter in a puddle of blood. "What now?"

"We tried to bring him in, but he pulled a gun on us. He killed Colter, but I got him, George. I got him," Middleton said, groaning. "I'm bleeding bad," he whimpered and passed out.

George picked two men and told them to take the big deputy to Doc Winters' place, then went into the store. He closed and locked the door, pulled the shades, and came out ten minutes later. Those on the street talked and chattered, many asking what the sheriff was doing inside the store, but got quiet when Sheridan George came out. He had Colter's and Jenkins' bodies taken for burial, and strolled through town to the Hearts of Gold Saloon.

"Here's Jenkins' copy of the mortgage, Holiday. We'll have to wait on setting up Dave Peterson. Jenkins was pretty damn fast. Killed Colter before he could pull leather, and shot Iron Mike after he was already dead," he said, laughing and slapping the bar. "Wonder if old Doc Winters will cut off his leg, too," his almost maniacal laughter echoing through the saloon.

Holiday finally told him to "shut up, you sound like an idiot. Let's go upstairs and talk. Too many ears down here," and they climbed the stairs to Holiday's office. He poured a couple from the good bottle and got right to business.

"Losing Colter isn't that big a loss, but right now, you have nobody on hand to pull off these next few jobs. Damn," he said, as he paced about in the spacious office. "You'll have to do Peterson by yourself. Shouldn't be hard, he's a little past just backward."

"Anybody making noise?" George asked, taking his whiskey down in a gulp, bringing a frown from Holiday.

"That's sippin' whiskey, George," he said, pouring another for him. "Only worried about what Quimby is up to. Governor can't do anything; I'm not worried about that. Right now, I own fifty percent of the bank and you and Swanson each own twenty-five. It's the same with the Morton Ranch, and now with the Emporium. I have men out at Morton's now, so that ranch will produce well, the bank is making money, and we will have to put someone in to run the Emporium.

"There are two big places I want. I want Sloan's ranch and I want the stockyards. Tonight, George, take out Peterson, and it's also time to start to intimidate that Flannigan woman. Run her red head right out of Plainsville. You're out of deputies. Go hire some of my men downstairs, but stay away from Cooper. He's a moneymaker on that table of his."

George's attitude had changed when he came back onto the saloon's main floor. He was grim, and he had questions that Holiday would not answer. *So the bank is making money. All banks make money, that's why we rob them. He wants some of his men to run a ranch when what they do is rustle cattle? I'm going to have to have it out with him. Tomorrow. I'll face him down tomorrow.* The thoughts wouldn't go away, though, despite several shots of whiskey.

"What're you lookin' at?" he snarled at the young bartender. "You got somethin' to say to me, spit it out," and he was fondling the worn wooden handle of his revolver. The bartender just nodded at the sheriff and walked down the bar, leaving Sheridan George to stew in his own bile.

Chapter Nine

P ete Quimby, after a cross-country stretch of a few miles, reached the Santa Fé Road, and put the big thoroughbred into a trot that ate miles. He checked the strong horse's heart and breathing regularly, slowed to a walk for a spell, then back to the trot and watched miles of New Mexico Territory pass by. "Looks like we got away with it," he said, checking behind him regularly. "Ain't no sense trying to hide my trail, since anyone following would know where I'm going," he said with a smile.

As the miles fell away he allowed his mind to relax a little. *Feels good to know I'm going to be in a camp, sleeping on the ground, listening for coyotes or wolves, not some fool getting drunk in a saloon, shooting up nothing but air. It's been a long time. Haven't had venison in the salt barrel for more than two years, don't seem to ever get away from the yards, and now, fighting these foul people looking to destroy all of our lives.*

His mind stayed alive through the rest of the day, enjoying desert scenes as they unfolded. He rode through them, found he had to ford a wash or two, still running from spring thaw, chased up a small group of antelope, some early hunting coyotes, and always, ravens looking for their next meal.

He rode well into sunset and moved off the trail and alongside a dry wash still filled with puddles from the long winter, and made a cold camp. He watered the horse and hobbled him in some early spring grass, ate smoked meat and cold biscuits, and rolled up in a wool blanket, letting his head rest on his duster, folded as a pillow.

Haven't seen this many stars in a long time, he thought. As his body slowly started the long resting cycle, his mind didn't, with too many thoughts about Holiday and George, outlaws and fraud keeping him awake. He wanted a plan and couldn't put one together, he wanted to meet the governor and have something positive in mind, and didn't. *Holiday came to Plainsville for a reason,* he thought, watching a shooting star skim through the black night. *What would bring an outlaw to our little town? There was no bank to rob, no major business or rich somebody to rob or steal from.* There simply were no answers, and he finally just closed his eyes, thought about enlarging his stockyards, creating a real town, and finally, slept like a log. He was back on the road before sunrise, he and his horse well rested.

"Should be just over the hill, Pard," he said to the horse, as he slowed him to a nice walk. "Santa Fé," he said, probably just to hear his own voice. "Been here for a long time, this old town has. Indians, Spanish, Mexicans, and now, Americans, all calling it the capitol." He walked his horse into town, enjoyed the sights of the old adobe buildings, and bustle of people and animals. "It'll be like this in Plainsville when that railroad starts coming through town," he mused, heard music that seemed to flow from every open doorway and balcony, and pulled up in front of one of the many livery stables in the old town.

He didn't dismount immediately, enthralled with the vista of the ancient town, the flavor and aroma of living history. *Spanish Conquistadores may have been on their horses exactly where I'm sitting on mine,* he thought, *and ancient Indian tribes may have held ceremonial feasts on this exact spot. Rose calls me a romantic and its times like this that I have to agree with her,* he smiled to himself, and saw the livery operator walk toward him.

"We've had a long ride, Mr. Blacksmith," he said, as he stepped out of the saddle. "This old boy needs a few day's rest, and so does my horse," he chuckled through his soft southern drawl. "Give him the best you've got and aim me toward a good hotel. Name's Quimby, Pete Quimby. How much?"

"That's one fine horse, Mr. Quimby. Dollar a day

will get him hay, oats, and water. More if he needs shoes or exercise."

"Here's five dollars, don't know if I'll be here that long. His shoes are fine and he's just gotten as much exercise as he wants or needs." He pulled the pack off the back of the saddle, took the rifle from its scabbard, and handed the lead to the big blacksmith.

"That a Henry?" the livery hand asked.

"Sure is. Old Ben Henry's .44 rimfire. Best rifle I've ever held in my hands. Now, sir, about that hotel."

"Hacienda de Santa Fé is right over there, Mr. Quimby. Fine hotel, good food, and a saloon attached. Thank you," he said, tossing the five dollar gold piece in the air and catching it. He led the big horse into the barn and Quimby threw the pack over a shoulder, carried the rifle with ease and walked to the hotel.

"If these streets could talk," he mumbled. "A pueblo before white men were ever around, then swarms of Spanish Conquistadores and horses. Imagine," he mused, kicking up ancient dust as he walked, "all those ancient people living life in this desert and not even knowing that such a thing as a horse existed. Must have been quite a sight when they first saw the Spanish."

He stopped just short of the boardwalk in front of the Hacienda de Santa Fé, admiring the old building. Adobe for the most part, with large timbers showing where a second floor had been added, and the deep set windows that helped cool the rooms in the summer and kept heat in in the winter. Quimby was wearing a big smile as he walked into the hotel lobby.

"Buenos Diaz, hello," the clerk behind the ornate counter said. "Been on the trail for a while?" he asked in a friendly manner.

"Just a couple of days, but a hard ride. Hope you have a room with a good bed for these tired old bones."

"For you, señor, only the best. Would you be Pete

Quimby?"

Quimby's head jerked straight up at the question. "Yes," he drawled out slowly, giving the clerk a long look, checking to see if anyone else was near. "I would be. How would you know that?" He was on full alert at the question. Did Holiday have someone in town to kill him? Was he actually followed, and they were waiting? He reached down and released the leather thong from the hammer on his revolver.

"No, no, señor, there is no problem," the clerk said, looking at Quimby's hand as it closed on the revolver's handle. "I have a letter for you from Governor Monahan," and he brought a large envelope from behind the counter. "We expected you later today. You have made good time, sir."

"How would the governor know I would come to this hotel?" he asked, wondering still if this wasn't a set up.

"He alerted all the liveries to watch for you and direct you here. Seems you have many friends in Territorial government, Mr. Quimby."

"Umm. Yeah," Quimby muttered. He picked up the key to room 107, along with the large envelope, hoisted his pack and rifle, and headed down the corridor to his room. "No more surprises," he said over his shoulder to the clerk, and caught a smile from the friendly man. "My first chore was going to be to empty a barrel of cold beer," he muttered, arranging things in the room, "but that isn't gonna happen. Yet," he said.

He sat on the bed and opened the envelope. "Dear Mr. Quimby," he read, "I have received several telegrams from Rose Flannigan, a long time friend, detailing many problems some of you people in Plainsville are having. I'm not sure at the moment what I might be able to do, but I very much want to hear your story and see if something can't be arranged.

"Please come to my office the morning after you

arrive in our fine little town, at ten o'clock. Rose had many good things to say about you and I'm looking forward to meeting you. Rose and her late husband were good friends in years past.

"Sincerely, James P. Monahan, Governor, Territory of New Mexico."

"Makes it easy," he thought, as he pulled his boots off and stretched out on the bed. He had just a short nap in mind but it was two hours later that he was awakened by a knock on the hotel door. Revolver in hand he said, "Who is it?"

"Name's Red Feather," the voice answered. "The governor asked me to stop by."

"Stand back from the door while I open it," Quimby said, unlocking the door and letting it swing open. He was standing to the side, gun in hand when a tall, husky Indian walked in. "Just ease over there while I catch the door," Quimby said, giving the man plenty of room.

Red Feather wore canvas britches and a buckskin shirt. He had high legging style moccasins, beautifully beaded. His gun belt, also well beaded, held a large Colt on one side and a Bowie knife on the other. "So, Mr. Red Feather, exactly what did the governor say to you?"

"My white name is Jose Red Feather, so just call me Jose or Joe or Red Feather. Don't get along much with the mister stuff," he smiled, sitting in one of the chairs. "Governor Monahan has been working with ranchers around the territory, particularly in the eastern parts, where cattle rustling has been rampant. He thought maybe we should have a chat before you see him.

"Mind if I light a cheroot?" he asked, pulling one from a buckskin pouch he wore around his neck. Quimby nodded, and Red Feather continued. "The Texans and Texians have been coming into the territory and rustling hundreds of steers and heifers regularly, and the ranchers want the territory to do something about it.

"Is that part of the problem you're having in Plainsville. You're quite a ways from the border, though."

Quimby enjoyed watching the man talk and hearing an almost musical way he had with words. The English language was obviously not his home language, but he spoke very well. His eyes shone with life, his face and body animated as he talked, and Quimby had a good feeling about the man.

He wore his hair long, parted slightly off center, braided, and plaited with ties of ornamental yarn. His hands were broad with long tapered fingers. While appearing casual, almost slouched in his chair, Quimby saw strength and agility, and in his eyes, a determination that told him he could trust the man.

"No," Quimby said, "our problem isn't rustling. I think we could handle that. A gang of outlaws has come to town, with lots of money behind them, and is trying to take over the town. We tried to have an election and with fraud and deceit they stole the ballot box, or stuffed it, I guess would be more correct." He paused to get his thoughts going in the right direction.

"They actually opened their own bank, have offered mortgages that are filled with duplicity, and have one of their own acting as sheriff. We need help," Quimby said, as he slumped onto the edge of the bed. He wasn't giving up but he simply had no answers, and appeared as a broken man.

"Do you drink beer, Mr. Quimby?" Red Feather asked, catching Pete by surprise.

"First, Red Feather, call me Pete, and second, yes," and the two stood up in unison. Quimby found his boots and hat, and the two headed out the door. *Looks like I'll have help with that barrel of beer,* he thought as they made their way onto the street. "You work for the governor?" Quimby asked, as they slipped into the saloon, the next-door neighbor to the hotel.

"The governor is trying to put together a territorial mounted police force to help end the rustling that's going on. So far," and he laughed at this, "there are three of us." He looked at Quimby long and hard, drank a draught of beer, and said, "Tell me about these outlaws in Plainsville. I've worked with law agencies around the west for several years. I might know some of these bad men of yours."

"Let's take our drinks to a table," Quimby said. "I'm not sure if I was followed or not, and there are lots of ears in here." They found a table near the front windows. "I love the way this town looks," Pete said. "Full of life, picturesque, rough and tumble. This is how I want Plainsville to end up."

For the next hour, the two sat drinking beer, talking back and forth as Quimby told about Thornton Holiday and Sheridan George, and the many outlaws that had come into town, to work for Holiday. He told how the election fraud took place, how a rancher had been killed. "That killing was a pure set-up, Red Feather. But in all of this, somewhere, the question of why has to be answered. We know what they're doing, but without knowing why they're doing these things, we can't really fight them.

"One of our ranchers, his name is Charlie Sloan, thinks we should just put together a vigilante type group and take the outlaws on, run 'em out of town or put them in graves. I don't think that's the right way."

"You have a lot of problems, Pete," Red Feather said as they got up to leave the saloon. "That man Sloan might be on to something, though. Townspeople and ranchers, led by real lawmen, would have the letter of the law behind them, and could get the job done.

"Talk to the governor tomorrow, and then I want to talk some more with you. I might just know some of these men you're dealing with. One in particular has been in my craw for a long time."

Pete Quimby said goodbye to Red Feather and spent

the next couple of hours just walking around Santa Fé, taking in all the sounds, sights, and smells of the ancient city. He bought a lovely mantilla for Rose, *There's that romantic me, again,* he said to himself, finally working his way back to the hotel and supper. He stopped at the desk first. "I love your city," he said to the clerk, "but a man could get lost real fast with all these little streets and lanes going every direction.

"I have to meet with the governor tomorrow morning and I have no idea where I would find him."

The clerk offered a knowing smile as he answered. "Walk out the front door of the hotel, turn right, and go to the end of the street. There's a large white adobe building on your right. You'll find the governor in there."

"A large, white adobe. I'll find it," Quimby said. "No visitors," he said with a smile and strolled down the hallway to his room. He washed up, thought about shaving and set that idea aside, and went back out to find the restaurant. Instead of the hotel's café, he headed down the street to a Mexican cantina.

I've been enjoying the aroma from this place since I got in town. If it's half as good as it smells, I found a new home. It was several hours before a sated Pete Quimby found his way back to the hotel, humming some plaintive Mexican song. *Rose should hire a Mexican lady to run that café,* were his last thoughts as sleep came fast.

***

Bill Pitts and Rose Flannigan were in the café, joined by Dave Peterson and Charlie Sloan. "Pete's in Santa Fé," Rose said, "and should be meeting with Governor Monahan in the morning. His wire said he wasn't followed, that he knows of, and not to worry.

"Not to worry," she snorted. "John Morton gunned down like a common criminal, Don Jenkins murdered in his own store, and that fool Sheridan George parading around like the ass he is." There was a fresh pot of coffee on the table along with a bottle of good brandy, and an Irish temper ready to explode.

Rose poured a hefty shot of brandy and topped the cup off with a bit of coffee, and continued. "Both Morton and Jenkins had that strange chapter in their mortgage, giving everything to the bank if they should die before their mortgage is paid off." She sat back for a minute, anger raging across her lovely face. "Bill, you showed me your mortgage, and that phrase isn't there. And Charlie, you said your paperwork didn't have that clause. How about you, Dave?"

"I don't read very well, Mrs. Flannigan," Peterson said, handing his papers to Rose. "Maybe you can read this for me?" He was slightly embarrassed, worked to hide that by getting another taste of brandy in his cup. "Grew up pushing cattle all over Texas and fightin' Indians. Not much chance for book learnin'," he said.

Rose went through the papers quickly. "No such clause in your contract either. I find it strange that the two dead men have that phrase, but none of you three do." Pitts, Sloan, and Peterson just sat there, not speaking, not knowing even what to say. After a long minute of silence, Rose said, "Well, we'll just have to wait until Pete gets back with whatever help the governor can give us."

Sloan looked around the table, scratching at stubble of beard. "You said the banker would show you his to copy of Morton's loan papers, but has anyone seen John's copy? Is it possible that a second copy would be different from the front copy?" He was answered by silence as the implication of what he said sank in.

"No matter what my copy says, if the bank's copy is different, and if I'm dead, and no one sees my copy, Holiday and the bank win." Anger and frustration were obvious as the group looked at each other, at the table, at the ceiling.

Pitts and Peterson left immediately, saying they had

work to do. "Rose, we've been friends ever since you came to this country, even helped me a couple of times after I lost Ruthie from the fever." Charlie Sloan was a worried man. He had his thumbs hooked in his belt, staring at the floor.

"These men don't play by anyone's rules but their own. I want to bring you my copy of the mortgage and have you keep it in your safe. I don't have any family, same as old John Morton and Mr. Jenkins, and that seems to be very important to Holiday. Will you do that?"

"I think that's the best idea I've heard in a long time, Charlie. Yes, bring it in tomorrow. The bank has offered their copies of Morton's and Jenkins' loan papers, but no one has seen the originals. They are stealing this land, this business, only because neither Morton nor Jenkins has any known relatives."

"That's the position I'm in, too, Rose," Charlie said. "I'll bring those papers in, and maybe we should talk to Peterson and Pitts, about theirs." He stood a little taller walking out the door, and down the street to the livery to reclaim his horse for the ride back to his ranch.

I need to get word to Reynaldo that Dave Peterson might be in Holiday's sights. He too is single, and someone needs to have possession of his mortgage papers, she was thinking, and wondering at the same time where Pete Quimby might have his papers stored.

***

At sunrise a lone cowboy came racing into town, sliding his horse to a stop in front of the Pitts Livery and Blacksmith facility. "Bill," he called, "Bill, where are you?"

"I'm right here, Reynaldo," Pitts answered, coming out from the stables. "What on earth is wrong?"

"Rustlers, Bill, rustlers. They took about fifty steers from Peterson, and killed the boss doing it. Where's the sheriff? We need to get a posse up and get Peterson's cattle

96

back. They killed old Randy and Peterson. I hit one, I think, but they rode in so hard, so fast, nobody had time to react."

Pitts held his horse while Reynaldo Cortez ran down the street to the Sheriff's Office. He burst through the door, howling that rustlers had killed Peterson and Randy Sharp. George calmed the man down some and said he'd get a posse up. "No need to ride with us, Rey," he said, motioning Iron Mike Middleton to get a couple of men from the saloon, and they would ride out immediately.

Cortez walked back to the livery to reclaim his horse. "Sheriff said I shouldn't join the posse. That seems strange to me, Pitts," he said. "I've been cow boss for Dave Peterson for several years. I should be in that posse." He and Pitts watched as George, Middleton, and three others rode out of town.

"Not one of them men knows the first thing about cattle," Cortez said. "If they do catch the rustlers, what are they gonna do with the herd? There are five men, not a cowboy in the bunch, and they don't want me with them." He shook his head in disbelief, gathered the reins and mounted the cow pony. "I'm going anyway," he said, touching the horse with his spurs.

Young Joshua came out of the barn as Cortez rode off. "Pop, I just heard something really strange." He was scuffing his boot toe in the dust, looked like a little boy who might have grabbed a cookie before asking.

"What, son?" Bill Pitts asked, walking toward the hot forge to do some ironwork. "You look bothered, pal. What happened?"

"I was near the saloon a few minutes ago, coming back from taking Mr. O'Reilly's horse back to him, when I heard that Middleton man say that he needed a couple of men to ride out of town with him."

"They just left, Josh. Peterson's cattle were rustled last night. They're going to try to catch the thieves."

"No, they're not!" Joshua barked. "Middleton said

he and the men would ride out to the ranch, gather up the dead bodies, and come right back to town. One of the men asked a question and Middleton got really angry.

"He said there wasn't any rustling, the cows are all still there. He said, 'We'll ride out, get the bodies, come back, and tell people that the rustlers got away, we saved the herd, and that's it.' Doesn't seem right, Pa," Joshua said, again poking around the dust with his boot toe.

"No, it doesn't," Pitts said, tousling his son's hair. "Why don't we walk down to the café, I think Rose Flannigan will want to hear what you have to say. You can have a cinnamon roll and some milk, and I'll have some hot coffee." The two walked down toward the hotel building as longtime friends as well as father and son.

"You have a knack for being in the right place, pal," Pitts said. "It sure sounds like Sheridan George and Thornton Holiday have pulled off another outright murder and land grab." As a second thought came into his head, he continued. "I wonder what Pete Quimby would do if he were in town?"

Chapter Ten

"Mr. Quimby, the Governor will see you now. Please follow me," the young man said, standing from his reception desk in the territorial capitol. He led Quimby down a hallway carpeted in rich wool and magnificent colors, the walls paneled in oak and walnut, gas lamps lit to fend off the darkness. Quimby had awakened that morning with a sense of unease, worried through the night that the governor would offer nothing, or worse, suggest that Plainsville deserved what it was getting.

The building was gorgeous, and he felt twinges of anxiety. *I should have brought better clothes,* he said, noting the young man's fine, clean, business wear, and his own workpants, clean shirt, and plainsman's jacket. *I'm about to meet the governor and I look like I should be herding cattle.*

The governor's office was equally fine as they entered; Governor James P. Monahan was behind his desk and stood to greet them.

Monahan was much older than Quimby expected, but had a firm grip when they shook hands. He stood well over six feet tall, had flowing white hair, brilliant blue eyes, and sported exceptional muttonchops, also snow white. Quimby remembered Rose telling him the governor had been a judge when she knew him. *He would be an impressive judge,* he thought, taking the seat offered him, then almost chuckling, *He is an impressive governor.*

The governor's demeanor spoke of leadership, from carriage to dress, but his actions were very personal, open, and friendly. Many territorial governors were placed by friendly presidents and congressmen as political payoffs, and even if this were the case in Monahan's background, Quimby was thinking, the man fit the description of governor of a territory still considered on the open frontier.

"Between the telegrams I've received from Mrs. Flannigan, and the conversation I had with Joe Red Feather last night, I'd say you have a heap of trouble in Plainsville. As I said before, though, I'm not sure what the Territorial Governor can do to help." He sat back in his massive, leather-bound chair behind the desk, drumming his fingers on the pile of papers in front of him, the telegrams and notes about the problem.

"We do have rules and laws governing elections, but the one thing we don't have is a means of enforcing those rules and laws. We have a territorial judiciary of sorts, we even have a territorial attorney general, but he can't act unless charges are brought, and I'm afraid in the case of Plainsville, whatever charges might seem warranted, there is no one to bring them.

"The biggest problem I see is that Plainsville simply doesn't exist. There is no township; even the county is in question. I'm really not sure what this office can do?"

"I'm not either, Mr. Governor," Quimby answered, "but since they elected their own sheriff and seem to be attempting to steal, by way of murder, much of the property and ranches, there should be some way to enforce territorial law. That is what I'm looking for. Some way to stop them, legally, and with the authority of the territory."

He paused briefly, and then continued. "One of the ranchers, a long time resident of the area is prodding the other ranchers to form a committee and simply ride the outlaws out of the area. Vigilante justice he calls it, but in my opinion, just as criminal as what Holiday and his gang are doing."

The pause wasn't too long, both men giving deep thought to the issue, and Quimby continued. "In some areas, vigilante groups form and take matters into their own hands, but I don't want that to happen in Plainsville. Not that it hasn't been discussed, but the ranches are well out of town, the business men are not fighters and gunmen, and we all want to do whatever needs to be done, legally."

"Vigilante law is never the right way, Mr. Quimby. Red Feather may have told you that I have been working to establish some form of territorial law enforcement. We don't have rangers like Texas, or territory-wide marshals as other areas," and he uttered an ironic chuckle, "we don't even have any money to establish such a service.

"But again, there are laws, federal and territorial, that have been broken in Plainsville, and I do have the authority to appoint investigators that would carry the authority of the territory. Red Feather works for me under those auspices," he said. "Would you accept a territorial appointment as Red Feather's Plainsville deputy, and with his help, clean up the problem? You must realize, too, there is no pay, just a tin badge gilded in danger."

Quimby's heart missed a beat or two as a smile slowly spread across his broad face. He stood up and reached across the wide mahogany governor's desk. "Thank you, Mr. Governor. I think you just hit on the answer." They stood, shaking hands for several seconds, and Governor Monahan walked Quimby to the door.

"I'll have Red Feather come to your hotel this afternoon, and the two of you will be on your own. I wish I had a platoon of men to send with you." The governor stood for a moment, in apparent thought. "One thing I think must happen as soon as possible. Right now, Plainsville is just a name. There is a place, but it is not a recognized town or village. You must form a town, create township laws and rules, and elect those that will serve the citizens of Plainsville Township. I'll have the Territorial Secretary forward all the necessary information to Rose Flannigan.

"This, I think, will give you, as a Territorial Investigator, even more authority. Good luck to you, and please, give Rose my best. My office is open to you at anytime, Mr. Quimby," and Quimby headed back to the hotel, his head filled with plans and thoughts about putting

Holiday and company out of business.

In less than an hour, Governor Monahan has possibly found the answer to our problems, he thought, stopping at the telegraph office to wire Rose Flannigan the good news. He was emphatic, telling her not to mention a word of this to anyone. He closed off the wire with the governor's good wishes.

If Holiday gets word of this appointment, he thought, walking back to the hotel, *I will never get back to Plainsville alive, and Rose, along with many more will be in even more dangers. Hopefully, old Tater will keep his fool mouth closed, as well.*

Quimby was in the hotel café having a late lunch when Red Feather arrived, both men smiling and greeting each other. "I have some papers you have to sign, a pledge you must make, and a tin badge that hopefully will help us get things in Plainsville taken care of," Red Feather offered, sitting down at the table. "Governor Monahan was impressed, Pete, and he's not often. I think we'll make a good team."

"This certainly won't be an easy task, Red Feather. Holiday is fairly well entrenched and has a stable of gunfighters on hand, and probably more that he can call on. I sent a telegraph to Rose. She needs to know that there is hope for all of us."

"I'm afraid of that, Pete. If word gets out, they will be laying for us on the trail. Telegraph operators are notoriously bad at spreading secret information, let alone rumors." He sat back, quietly absorbing what Quimby had said. "Let's go up to your room, do some long range planning, and hit the trail before sunup tomorrow."

Quimby was certain that Rose would not say a word to anyone, but what Red Feather said about telegraph operators brought questions about Plainsville's Tater. He was known for letting slip what was in a personal cable. *I better start thinking from a broader point of view* he thought, leaving the café.

***

Cortez spotted the posse just minutes out of Plainsville, moving along at just a walk. He pulled his horse up, slowed to a walk, and started a long conversation with his horse. "A posse chasing cattle rustlers doesn't just walk along a trail," he said. "And they would want a capable cowman along with them."

He trailed well behind the posse, staying out of sight and watching the trail they were leaving. As he approached the ranch, he dropped into an arroyo and tied his horse off, creeping as close as he dared to the group. *What the hell are they up to?* He wondered, worming his way through the dust and underbrush, trying to get close enough to see what was going on.

"Get them cows back here as best you can," Sheriff Sheridan George said to what Cortez thought were the rustlers. "Middleton, you and Slim gather the bodies and make them ready for the ride back." He glared at Middleton, saying, "Tie 'em off good this time. I'm going to go through the ranch house. We should be ready to head back to town within the hour." George headed for the ranch house and Cortez moved cautiously back to his horse, and another fast ride back to Plainsville.

He pulled his heavily lathered horse to a halt in front of the livery, bailing off before it was fully stopped. "Pitts," he hollered, "Pitts, where are you?"

Young Josh stepped out of the stables. "Pa's down at the hotel talking with Mrs. Flannigan. I'll take care of your horse, Mr. Cortez."

"Thank you, Josh," Reynaldo yelled, as he raced down the dusty street and blasted through the doors of the hotel. "Pitts in here?" he howled at Sorenson behind the counter.

"In the office," Sorenson said, and Reynaldo Cortez strode down the hallway, burst through the office door, out

103

of breath, speaking faster than they could understand. Half of it was in Spanish, some in English, some a mixture of the two.

"Slow down, Rey," Rose Flannigan said. "What on earth is the matter? Bill, talk to him while I get some coffee. He needs something."

Bill Pitts listened to Cortez and knew already what had happened, because of what his son Josh had told him. "I know Rey," he said. "Josh heard the sheriff tell Middleton how to handle the so-called rustling. I wish I knew what to do about it. I wish Pete Quimby were here."

Flannigan walked in at that moment. "We all do, Bill. Here, Rey, I put a drop or two of brandy in the coffee. That'll fix you up."

Reynaldo had caught his breath, gave Rose a big smile and took a long drink. "Whoa," he said, "if that's a drop or two, you can do this anytime you like," he said, laughing, taking another drink. "So, the entire rustling, the killing of Dave Peterson and Randy, was a set up so the bank will own the property? That's amazing, Bill, Rose. How can they get away with that?"

"Because there's no one here to stop them," Rose Flannigan snarled. "Hired outlaws, gunslingers, murderers, thieves, and right now, they run things around here. Bill, I saw Dave Peterson's loan papers the other night, and there was no clause in that contract that called for the bank to own the property if Peterson should die before the loan is paid off.

"If that miserable banker comes up with papers that say it does, they will be forged. I will demand to see them."

"That could get you killed, Rose," Bill Pitts said, filling all the cups, half coffee, half brandy. "I think we need to wait for Pete Quimby before trying to do anything. We can't go up against hired guns, and that George would shoot you just because he knows he can. We need to keep ourselves as safe as possible and wait for Quimby," he said, draining his cup. "I'm going to stick close to the livery, work to keep Josh safe, and wait."

Before Reynaldo could follow Bill Pitts out, Rose asked him to stay. "I have Old Pete behind the bar in the saloon and little Gerald Sorenson behind the desk in the hotel, and that's it, Rey," she said, her lower lip quivering in fright. "I think you just lost your job at the Peterson Ranch, so how about going to work for me as full-time security. You're pretty handy with guns.

"That man Holiday has a hatred for Pete and me, he would kill me or have me killed the minute it appears I'm vulnerable. Are you as handy with your guns as you are with your fists?" she asked, remembering Fourth of July boxing matches in which Reynaldo Cortez won most of the time.

"I am, Rose, and it would be my pleasure to work for you. Mr. Peterson was a fine man, a true cowman. He built a wonderful ranch, good breeding stock, and more on the way. He doesn't have any relatives that I know of, and always said that if he died, the main group of employees should take over the operation.

"You're right, I'm out of a job, out of part ownership of a fine ranch, and out of a wonderful friendship. Consider me hired," he said, sticking a gnarled hand out to Rose Flannigan.

Rose took the hand and then drew the lanky cowboy in close. "I feel much safer now," she said, holding him, rubbing his back, feeling his strength as he held her close. They stood, rocking back and forth, saying all the things they had been wanting to say for several months. "I've wanted a partner for a long time, Rey. It looks like I have a lot more than a business partner now."

"Isn't it wonderful, we have these warm, close feelings, and it was danger and chaos that brought them into the light." Reynaldo Cortez let his fingers caress her cheek, and her strong jaw line and chin. "I'm just a beat up old cowboy, Rose, and you're a lady. I hope I meet your standards."

"You're a big, strong man, Reynaldo Cortez, a gentleman, and right now, a knight in canvas pants and chaps, defending what is right in the world." They spent the next several hours planning the defense of the Plainsville Hotel and Red Rose Saloon.

Rose was in the Red Rose that evening when Charlie Sloan rode into town. "I heard some strange talk from some of my men, this afternoon, Rose. Said old Dave Peterson was killed by rustlers? And none of Peterson's cattle is missing? Something pretty strange."

Rose motioned to Old Pete to pour a round for them and she told the story. "Pete Quimby should be back in the next day or two, Charlie. I don't think there's much we can do before then."

"I brought those papers from the bank," he said, taking a long drink from his glass. "Keep these locked up, Rose, just in case some rustlers come by my place," and there was no smile on anyone's face. "I'm going to spread the word among all the cowboys that work on our ranches, that we may need to protect ourselves. I was going to stay in town tonight, but I think I'll head back to the ranch." He drained his whiskey, nodded goodnight to all, and walked straight and tall out the door.

"He may have the right idea," Rose muttered, draining her drink as well. "I'm glad I have Reynaldo." She walked back to office, took Sloan's copy of his mortgage and tucked it safely in the big steel safe, along with the copy of Quimby's papers. *Peterson's mortgage didn't have that ugly clause, and he was killed anyway,* she thought, sitting at her small desk. *Neither do Sloan's or Quimby's. I don't have a copy of Peterson's mortgage, but I do the other two. That puts me at the wrong end of a high-powered rifle,* and she felt a shiver run up and down her back. "Come on, Pete," she said aloud, "get your butt back here, where you belong."

Rose Flannigan and Reynaldo Cortez took adjoining rooms on the second floor of the hotel, and were talking late into the evening. "I brought several of the Peterson hands into town, Rose," Cortez said. "They will be working as security guards inside and around the outside of the hotel and saloon. You can sleep in peace, my lady."

***

Holiday and George were locked in Holiday's office, both angry and loud. "Your men allowed the Peterson Ranch foreman to get away, and now the whole town knows the rustling was a set-up," Holiday was bellowing with rage. "No survivors," he growled. "No witnesses. What the hell is so hard to understand? The only way this works is if there are no witnesses, no one alive to tell the tale. Sheridan, you have let me down."

Sheridan George was just as livid as Holiday. "Those were your men, Holiday," he stormed. "You picked them, you gave them their orders. You fouled the play, not me. Don't ever talk to me again in that tone of voice or I'll splash your brains all over this nice office," and he stomped toward the door, then whirled to face Holiday.

"By the way, Tater, at the telegraph office says Quimby is coming back, wearing a territorial star." He unlocked the door and started out.

"Wait. Wait, George. Maybe I am too quick to criticize. You're right, those were my men, and I did give them their orders. There's just so much at stake." He picked up a bottle of fine whiskey and poured two glasses, offering one to George. "Can you speed up our plan, take out that red head?

"And, you said Tater gave you that information? Find out what else he knows, anyway you can, using whatever means necessary. Take out that Flannigan woman tonight, and we'll get Quimby when he gets back to town. My plan, and it's working, Sheridan, it's working, is going to keep us rolling in gold coin for the rest of our lives. This isn't the time to let things fall apart."

Sheridan George moved slowly toward the desk, still boiling angry, took the offered drink and downed it in one swallow, more to get Holiday's goat than anything, and said he'd get right on it. "She'll be gone by dawn," he barked, and walked out the door.

Holiday stood up and walked to the fire, letting the hot coals mix with the hot bourbon, and let his dreams move through his head. *My first change will be to build a large, beautiful home for myself, in the European manner, and have servants to wait on my every need. I'll have to ease Sheridan out of his percentage, probably the banker as well. This is my plan, my kingdom; I make the rules.*

Chapter Eleven

Quimby and Red Feather rode out of Santa Fé a couple of hours before sunrise, Red Feather trailed a burro packed for the two or three day ride. "We'll go cross country, Pete. If Holiday knows we're coming, he'll expect us on the road. May take a little longer, but much safer."

"Do you have some kind of plan for when we get there?" Quimby asked, as he gnawed on a hard biscuit.

"I've never gotten along well being sneaky. I like being bold, and I think that would be our best bet. We'll ride straight into town, badges showing bright and shiny, and lay down the law." He had a grin on his face that told Pete there might just be a little more to it than that, and he took the bait.

"Ok," he said, "go on. I can feel there's a lot more to it than that."

"Maybe a little more," the lawman said. "We'll come in to town by way of some of the ranches, and it is possible that some of the ranchers, maybe even some of their hired hands will want to ride in with us. That would be nice," Red Feather said with a straight face for another couple of seconds.

"So," Quimby snorted, "If Sloan and his cowboys rode into town and chased Holiday and the gang out, that would be vigilante justice, but if those same cowboys were led by a couple of guys wearing badges, everything is just fine."

"Sounds reasonable to me," Red Feather quipped. Both men enjoyed a good laugh, and for the next many hours rode through mile after mile of New Mexico landscape. They rode through arroyos, some still with water standing, through desert without benefit of a marked trail, and saw very little wildlife. They took a break about mid-day in an arroyo that still held water that gave the animals time to drink and find some fresh grass that grew in the warm spring weather.

Red Feather filled a pot with the water and boiled it for several minutes before tossing some smoked venison in. Quimby opened a couple of hard biscuits and they dipped the bread in the soup and ate a hearty mid-day supper. "I miss this," Pete Quimby said, as he settled back on a pack, lighting a cheroot. "Used to get out two or three times a year like this. Bring venison home, antelope sometimes, and turkey. Smoked turkey, that's what I really miss."

"I rode with a horrible old sheriff up in Idaho for a couple of years, but that man followed the Snake River down to where the salmon came upstream, and he smoked some of the best fish I've ever had," Red Feather said. "That's in Nez Percé country. Fine horse people, they are."

An hour or so later they were re-saddled and re-packed and back on the trail. They spent the rest of the day discussing some of the problems they might face when they reached Plainsville. Quimby told about the people, who might help, who would or maybe could not, and gave him a fair layout of the town. They set up camp for the first night near a fair water hole that featured good grass, had a fire, and ate fresh meat and potatoes.

"Figure we probably should hit Charlie Sloan's ranch first. He has a fair size bunch of hands, then swing over to Peterson's. His foreman, Reynaldo Cortez will be a huge asset to us," Quimby said. "We should be able to ride into town with maybe ten or twelve men."

"We've made good time," Red Feather said. "If we can match today, we will be close to Plainsville late tomorrow. We're south of the Santa Fé Road. Will our present track bring us to those ranches?"

"No," Quimby said. "They would be north of the road, and a bit to the west."

"Alright, we'll angle north when we leave in the morning, and cross the road, before continuing west." He remembered crossing a road like that with five animals, not three like they had, and not leaving a trace for someone to see. "We'll brush it up good and hope nobody spots our crossing. I'm still worried that Holiday's people will be expecting us or riding to meet us."

They left camp early and rode in silence for hours, watching hawks and eagles dancing through thin air high above the desert, chased up a rabbit or two, some quail near the water holes, and kept an eye out for dust plumes. Mid-day meal was from saddle bags without benefit of stopping, making excellent time through the open country.

***

Sheridan George was in a foul mood following his meeting with Holiday. He slammed his way out of the saloon and stomped his way down the dusty street toward the Sheriff's Office. "Bring that telegraph guy here," he snarled to Mike Middleton, as he crashed through the door. "And, don't give me no back talk." He sat at his desk, pulled a bottle from a drawer and didn't bother with a glass. "Now, Middleton," he snarled when the one-armed deputy didn't move fast enough.

Middleton headed over to the telegraph office, closed by this time in the evening, and smashed the door open with his foot. He found Tater in his little apartment at the back of the building, having supper. He grabbed the old man, jerked him to his feet, and led him out the busted door, across the street, and pushed him into the office. Tater was squalling, crying, kicking, and made enough noise that several people were able to catch a glimpse of what was happening.

It took about five minutes for the word to reach Rose Flannigan. She and Reynaldo Cortez went downstairs and into the Red Rose Saloon. "Looks like my wires to Pete and his answers back will be known by George and Holiday," Flannigan said, as anger flowed like hot lava through her words. "I hope Pete gets back soon. This town is about to blow up, I'm afraid."

Cortez called a couple of men over. "Rose, these men are from Peterson's Ranch. They were run off by George and Middleton. This is Tyler," he said, and pointed to a tall, heavily built blonde man, just barely able to grow a mustache, "and this is Slim Owens." Owens was about six feet tall and didn't weigh one fifty fully dressed. "I have two other of our crew posted in the back of the hotel, near the doorway that leads to your carriage house."

Rose smiled warmly at Reynaldo Cortez, "Gentlemen, I'm so glad to meet you." She motioned to Old Pete to pour a round. "I'm afraid our war is about to start, so let's have a toast to success." Glasses clinked, and as the four of them took a drink, a gunshot rang out down the street. "I'm afraid Tater just died," she whimpered. "Those bastards will be coming for me, Rey. We have to be safe, be alive and ready to fight when Pete gets back to town.

"What kind of men are they?" she asked, knowing there would be no answer. "Tater, just an old man working the telegraph, and what did they do to him before they killed him? I may not be as strong as you, Rey, but right now, I could whip that Sheridan George and Mike Middleton without help." She was angry enough that her entire body was shaking, tears flooding her cheeks, eyes blazing their Irish background. Old Pete found himself backed as far from her as he could get.

"We need to get word to Sloan," Cortez said. "Somebody needs to ride fast and hard, to warn Charlie. Sheridan George has about five men at Peterson's, maybe three at Morton's old place, and Charlie Sloan has to be next."

"I know just the person," Rose said. "Let's the four of us take a little walk," and they downed their drinks and walked out the door and turned toward the livery. Josh and Bill Pitts were finishing supper when the four walked in the door.

"Did I hear a gunshot?" Pitts asked, standing up to greet his visitors.

Rose was astounded by the comment, thinking to herself, *Bill Pitts was Rudy Thomas's deputy and he hasn't reacted at all to a gunshot late at night in a town run by outlaws. Pete was right about him not being the right man for that job.*

What she said, though, was "I'm afraid so. We have a big problem, Bill, sit down so we can talk." Rose and Rey Cortez spent the next half-hour explaining what was probably about to happen, ending by asking the most important question Rose had ever contemplated.

"So, Bill," she said. "George and Holiday now know everything about Pete Quimby and the fact that he is now a territorial lawman and is coming back with help. I hate to ask this, but I have to. We need your gun in town, and we need to get word to Charlie Sloan as fast as possible to come to town and bring some of his crew with him."

Josh Pitts stood right up. "I'll go," he said. "I know the way to Charlie's ranch, and I can ride hard and fast." Bill Pitts started to say something, and Josh wouldn't let him.

"Dad," he said, loud and strong, "you let me run the mill, a man's job. You let me run the forge, make shoes, iron work, build wheels, a man's work. I'm only fourteen, but I'm doing a man's work, and this calls for a man to get Charlie Sloan. I'm going."

The silence only lasted a second or two, and Bill clapped his son on the shoulder, stuck out his hand, and said, "Yes, son, you are a man. Saddle Jake. Ride out the back of the stables, not the front, stay off the main road for at least a mile, then ride hell for leather." He chucked the boy under his chin. "I'm so damn proud of you," and he hugged him tight, and turned him toward the door.

Josh was gone in less than ten minutes; the dark of

night hid him in moments, the sound of the horse gone as well. "Adios," Cortez mumbled, as the group watched the boy disappear. They also heard someone running from the Heart of Gold Saloon down the main street to the sheriff's office.

"They won't catch Josh," Pitts said, "but it won't hurt to slow them down a bit. Help me push this freight wagon into the street, Reynaldo. With the livery on one side and the equipment shop over there, they won't get through. Even two or three minutes will be a good headstart for Josh." They pushed a huge freight wagon from the side of the livery into the middle of the street, and Rose brought out four horses, as if to fit them for harness. Pitts brought out the harness and laid it out, a set for one team at the front side of the wagon, and a set for the other team at the backside.

The road was effectively blocked, as Sheridan George and Iron Mike Middleton thundered down the street in the dark of night, pulling their horses to a hard skidding stop in front of the wagon. "Get this mess cleaned up," he howled, his horse churned tight circles, Middleton hung on to a rearing horse, almost getting throwed. The four large freight horses joined the show, breaking free and bucking, one kicked George, which brought another howl, this time of pain mixed with anger.

It was several minutes before the sheriff and his deputy were able to get their horses under control, and raced toward the saloon and around the other side of the livery, around the corrals and feed sheds, finding the northbound trail and taking up the chase. George stopped about two or three minutes later and stepped off his horse. He bent low to the ground, walked back and forth across the trail, and remounted.

"Might as well head back, Mike. Nobody rode out this way. Stony must have been mistaken. Probably the clatter of Pitts setting up the freight wagon." The two walked their horses back to town and were surprised to find the freight wagon parked alongside the livery, no horses or tack nearby. "Bastards," he snarled. The situation did not dawn on Middleton.

Cortez walked Rose Flannigan back to the hotel, got her settled, set up his people for the rest of the night, and took a position in his second floor room where he could sit in the dark and see up and down the dusty main road.

George had his pants leg rolled up, dabbing at a nasty, bloody gash in the side of his knee. He gritted his teeth and poured whiskey into the wound, wanting to howl like a wolf from the pain, but didn't, with Middleton looking on. He wrapped the wound with some torn fabric and tied it off. "Thanks for the help," he snarled at Middleton, hobbling to his desk, and drank the bottle of whiskey empty. "She dies tonight," he coughed, putting the bottle down. "Tonight."

"Why was that wagon in the street?" Middleton asked, pacing about the office. "Doesn't make much sense to me."

"Not to you, it wouldn't," George snarled, shaking his head. *One more word, Middleton,* the sheriff was thinking, *and first I shoot you, then Holiday.* "Get your dumb ass up to the saloon and bring Jesse Cooper here. I need at least one person here that can think. Bring one of Holiday's boys back with you too. Now git."

He didn't have a plan, but figured he would just have Middleton and Cooper bull his way through the hotel, ransack as much as possible, and finding Flannigan, kill her on sight.

***

Josh Pitts rode his horse hard and fast through the open desert, through some brush, over some, seldom around any, and found the main rode about a mile north of town. He let the horse walk for a few minutes to catch its breath, then put him in a long lope, eating up the miles.

There were lamps still burning when he pulled up at the main ranch building. He was off the horse, letting the reins fall to the ground, and bound through the gate and onto the porch.

"Mr. Sloan! Mr. Sloan," he yelled, banging on the heavy wooden door, which was yanked open immediately.

"What on earth?" Sloan said. "Josh, what brings you out this late, and just look at your horse, lathered."

Josh Pitts spilled out the story in one long stream of words as Sloan led him into the spacious living room of his ranch house. He settled Josh into a large leather chair in front of a blazing fire, the boy still talking a mile a minute. Charlie took it all in, brought a large pot of coffee in from the kitchen and settled into a chair next to young Pitts.

They talked for another hour and Sloan went out and had one of his men put Pitts' horse up. "Spread the word to the boys. As many as want to come, I'm needed in town. That phony sheriff and outlaws Holiday and Middleton are killing people and stealing property left and right. We'll leave at daybreak, and those that come, need to bring guns. Lots of them."

He walked back to the main house, thinking how best he and boys could help. *I think if we just show up, heavily armed and angry, those fools will back off. Quimby better hurry with his help, too.* It was a restless night for Sloan and Josh Pitts, and morning came too early.

Chapter Twelve

Quimby and Red Feather crossed the main road just as the sun broke through some scattered clouds, and headed toward Charlie Sloan's ranch. "We have made good time, Pete," Red Feather said, as he pointed out smoke in the distance. "That Sloan's place?"

"Sure is. We should be there in half an hour, and Peterson's spread is another couple of hours from there. Sloan's up early, looks like." They put their horses and burro into a little faster walk through open desert and arrived just as a large group of men were seen moving off the ranch at a lope.

"I'll catch them," Quimby said, handing the burro's lead rope to Red Feather. He put his horse into a full gallop and caught up within minutes. Sloan, young Pitts, Sloan's foreman, Tommy O'Rourke, and Quimby stepped off their horses and settled onto their haunches, while young Pitts gave his speech one more time. Red Feather arrived in time to hear most of it.

"That's just so hard to believe," Quimby said, shaking his head. "They tortured and killed Tater? They killed Peterson? I knew about Morton, but, my God, what are they expecting to gain? And you said they also killed Don Jenkins? What do you make of this Red Feather?"

"I've been working on an answer to that question from the time I read the original wire to the governor. This is how a dictator would take over a country, not how a criminal would rob and steal from a community. There's a level of intimidation here that I haven't seen in criminal activity. Holiday seems to be intimidating an entire community, and the answer will be found in answering the question, why.

"Somewhere these must be a reason behind all of this. In most criminal activity, once you understand where and how money fits the equation, you understand the crime and perpetrator." He rolled a smoke, giving each person a glance before continuing.

"What's to gain?" he asked. "Criminals work for something, and that something is what people like me use to capture them. Most of the time, that something is money, so what is Holiday working toward?

"If you kill a rancher and the ranch property transfers to a trust held by you and the bank? Most outlaws would simply rustle the herd. Why install a criminal, a known killer, as sheriff, and use him to kill the rancher? And the bank? Most criminals, again would simply rob a bank not build one." The big Indian sat comfortably on his haunches, letting his thoughts sink in.

"My initial thought was and is, Mr. Holiday has lost his mind, is very self-centered, and is setting up some kind of kingdom, as if there is no such thing as territorial or federal laws and statutes. This is how little kingdoms in Europe are created.

"I've chased outlaws and criminals all over the west, and I can't remember anything like what you have described. All outlaws only think of themselves, but this Thornton is out of his mind and self-centered to an extreme. That's more than just dangerous.

"We'll have to remember that, and keep in mind that Sheridan George is nothing but a murdering puppet and will do as he is told. Middleton probably still can't buckle his spurs."

Quimby sat still for just a couple of minutes before responding. "That is frightening to think about, Red Feather, but I certainly don't have any better thought on what and why this is happening. We've got a long ride into town, so better get back in the saddle, men."

The trail into Plainsville from the Sloan ranch went through some lovely country with magnificent mesas looming in the distance, grand vistas of desert on the one hand, and fine grass and feed for cattle on the other.

Surrounded by beauty on all sides, Quimby was thinking, passing through dips and rises in the open country, *and someone has to foul it up. Pastoral, that's what I'm thinking and we're riding into a nest of murdering thieves and outlaws.*

***

Middleton brought more than Jesse Cooper and a couple of toughs from the Hearts of Gold Saloon when he returned. Thornton Holiday was bristling when he walked into the office. "The whole damn village is aware of what you did and how you did it, Sheridan. What were you thinking?" he stormed, slamming the office door hard enough to shake the entire building. "Get the information, kill the wire operator, but not in front of the whole town."

"Who really cares?" George responded. "It's our town, no one will stand up to us, so who cares?"

"I'm trying to establish a refuge for every and all of the men we've ridden with over all these years, a place where they won't fear any lawman, where we can venture out to fill our pockets with gold, and I don't think you are working with me." Holiday was stammering some as he said this, anger boiling.

Sheridan could see something else as Holiday stormed about the office. *His eyes are those of a mad man,* he said to himself. *He's off his nut, and I gotta figure a way to get out of this. He thinks he's some kind of outlaw king, and he's gonna get all of us killed.*

"All right," Holiday finally said, settling into one of the cane chairs. He lit a cigar, still glaring at the sheriff. "Rose Flannigan must be put away, and we must make plans, be prepared for when Quimby gets here. Middleton said Quimby is bringing some kind of lawman from Santa Fé? What kind of lawman, George?"

"Tater said Quimby has been made some kind of Territorial Marshal, or something like that, and has another marshal with him. That's all I got out of him before

Middleton got angry and shot the fool. You need to back off, Holiday. I don't like the way you've been talking to me lately, and I don't understand this so called grand plan of yours, anyway.

"What the hell good is owning a bank going to do when we can rob any bank we want anywhere we go? What good is it going to do us to own ranches when if we want cattle all we have to do is rustle a herd? I think you've gone just a bit overboard on this power stuff. What are you trying to prove, that you're some kind of New Mexico outlaw king?" Sheridan George hit the answer without knowing it, Middleton and Cooper, along with a couple of tough guys, just stood listening to the two men, not having a clue.

Holiday just stared at the sheriff for a couple of minutes, then erupted, again. "You're a fool, Sheridan. I am creating a paradise for us. If you're not willing to follow this to its end, say so now," and he stood up, glaring, daring the huge man to try something.

Cooper broke the dangerous spell. "One of the cowboys from the Peterson Ranch was in the saloon, and is just drunk enough, we can use him to get to the Flannigan woman."

Holiday and George spoke almost at the same time. "How, so?" they said. Cooper said that Rose Flannigan would come to his aid if she thought he was in trouble, and then could be taken care of. "That's good, Cooper," Holiday said. "You and Middleton, go get him, charge him with anything you want, and Mike, if you kill him, I will kill you on sight."

***

"I would think that Pete will be coming in today sometime," Rose said to Reynaldo Cortez as they entered the café. "It was quiet last night following the shooting of Tater, but it won't be today, I'm afraid."

Cortez sat down, shaking his head. "One of my

men, Tyler, left his position behind the hotel last night, and Slim said he thinks he went to the Hearts of Gold Saloon. I hope not, but I haven't seen him this morning." He was contemplative, questions running through his mind. "I really anticipated an attack on you last night, not one of our boys not thinking."

"That's not good," Rose said, and poured coffee for the two of them. She was about to continue when Slim ran into the room.

"They're chasing Tyler," he said, out of breath. "Somebody at the saloon said Tyler cheated at the Faro table, and he ran."

"How long ago?" Cortez asked.

"Late last night. I just heard about it. Tyler shot one man in the saloon and raced out of town with some of the sheriff's deputies chasing him."

"That's the set-up they used on Morton," Cortez muttered. "Tyler might be more than they can handle, but in the meantime, we have to be ready for them to come after Rose. They can't let her live, and they have to get ready to head off Pete when he rides into town."

"Quimby can't get here soon enough, I'm afraid," Rose said. "Will he come in by the main road?" she asked, shaking her head. "What has happened to our wonderful little town? How can these men think they can just rob and kill and steal? We have to stop them," she whimpered.

"Slim, we can't wait for Pete Quimby. Here's what I want you to do," Reynaldo Cortez said. "Ride hard and fast to Charlie Sloan's place. Young Josh Pitts left out last night, but tell Sloan just how desperate we are here in town, tell him we need him and his whole crew in town just as soon as they can get here."

For the first time that morning, Rose Flannigan had a smile on her face. "Yes," was all she said as Slim left the café.

***

Three riders came around the bend in the trail, their tired horses walked slow, the men looking down at the trail in front of them to make sure they were still following Tyler's prints in the dust, then looked out in front, along the trail, hoping to spot the cowboy. Tyler was hidden behind a rock outcrop, and sighted down the long barrel of his Winchester, trying to decide which one of the three should go first.

The squeeze was long and slow and the hammer slammed down sending a big, heavy lead bullet through the chest of Iron Mike Middleton. One more time the hammer slapped steel, and this bullet pierced the heart of Jesse Cooper, gambler, Hearts of Gold Saloon and Dancehall.

"Don't move, stupid, and you might live," Tyler hollered down the slope from his perch. "Step off that bronc, slow and easy. Nice boy," he chuckled. "Drop that gunbelt and walk toward my voice. Ah, ah, now, I can see you clear as sweet honey through these sights, and I will kill you sure as hell if you make that wrong move. Now, walk," he snarled. "All the way up, nice and slow.

"You and Iron Mike think you're pretty damned clever, eh? Saying I robbed old Cooper there, and trying to chase me down. They's dead, and I'm right here." He stood up, the rifle cocked and aimed at the outlaw's chest. "Time for a chat, now. Just you and me."

The outlaw stepped around the rock and Tyler whacked him across the side of the head with the barrel of the Winchester. "Several good people in Plainsville have come up dead, their land coming into Holiday's holdings. You claim I cheated that table? That's what you bastards did to Morton? That's why old Peterson is dead? That why Holiday and that banker own so much property around here? Set your butt down. We gonna have us a pow-wow."

He took the man's side arm, found a knife in his boot, and cuffed him with the rifle barrel again, just because he could. "You're nothin' but a ugly outlaw, mister, and your two friends are gonna be stinking before we get them into town. I'm gonna march your skinny butt into the sheriff's office and make him tell me what you all have done to that town." And he whacked him again, opening a large wound across the side of his head.

"Now, load them dead bodies on them horses, good and tight, and the whole town is gonna watch you lead those dangerous outlaws through town. Move it," and the rifle came for another whack.

Two tired horses with two tired riders leading two tired horses with two dead riders rode into Plainsville about noon. Within minutes the four horses were tied off in front of the sheriff's office and a crowd had gathered. "Buenos Tardes, Sheriff," Tyler said. "Gotta couple of friends of yours here, and this other friend, wants to make a little speech." He jabbed the outlaw in the kidneys.

"Go on, now, tell your story."

"Wait a minute, there. Hold up, Tyler," Sheriff George said. "Let's get these bodies taken care of first. You men, take them over to the funeral parlor, and you men, get these horses some water and feed.

"Now, Mr. Tyler, what have you done? Let's go in the office, just the three of us, and have some coffee," and he opened the door to the little jailhouse that sat in the middle of the main block in the dusty village. Tyler wasn't in a thinking mood, neither Cortez nor Flannigan were there to tell him no, and he followed the sheriff into the office.

"You kill Iron Mike and the gambler?" Sheriff George barked when they were all seated. "You'll hang, Tyler. Those men are law dogs, Tyler, deputies. You'll hang."

"You lie," Tyler barked. "I didn't cheat any Faro table. You and that Holiday have been killing all the good people in this valley. He's no deputy, he's a killer and thief."

"He's lying, sheriff," the outlaw said, quietly, reaching for a cigar, biting the end off and accepting a light from George. "He robbed the gambler sure as I'm sitting here, and he killed those two. I saw him do it, in cold blood. Lined 'em up and shot 'em dead, he did," the outlaw lied, giving Tyler a big smile.

"I need to get back to the saloon, sheriff," he said, standing up, shaking George's hand, and walking out the door. "Come by later and we'll settle up." The sheriff followed him to the door and motioned one of the deputies to come inside.

As he turned around, he drew his revolver and shot Robert Tyler dead, walked to the body and pulled Tyler's Colt from its holster and forced it into his hand. "Damn fool thought he could out-draw me. You saw that, Jenner." The deputy nodded yes, called two more men into the jail to dispose of the body, pointing out the drawn weapon in Tyler's hand.

Those in the street hung their heads as Tyler's body was dragged from the office and roughly carted off to the undertaker. Rose Flannigan and Rey Cortez, just arrived, stood on the wooden sidewalk in front of the hotel, and watched in horror. "Who's next?" is all Rose could say.

"Let's get back to the saloon, Rose," Reynaldo said, taking the lady by the arm. He marched her onto the boardwalk, across from the jail, and up the street to the hotel. "I still have at least two men in town, and we need to get as much town help as we can inside the Red Rose Saloon."

Two men stepped out from the hotel entrance and held the door open for Rose and Cortez. "Go up and down the street, carefully, and bring as many men as will come back to the saloon. We need to hole up there until Quimby and Sloan arrive, and that could still be hours." He escorted Flannigan through the connecting doors into the saloon and motioned for Old Pete to set up a couple of glasses.

"If we're really lucky," Cortez said, "Sloan is already on his way and Slim will meet up with him. I just hope that Holiday hasn't sent men out on the main Santa Fé road to ambush Quimby." Rose sipped her whiskey and motioned Old Pete to come down to her end of the bar.

"How many guns do you have behind the bar, Pete?" she asked, getting a smile from both him and Cortez.

"I've got the two big scatter guns and two revolvers, Rose. Do you think Holiday will rush the saloon? Well, he'll get one hell of a surprise if he does."

Chapter Thirteen

S lim was pushing his horse hard through mostly open country on the trail to Sloan's ranch, and as he topped a slight rise he saw dust about a mile ahead of him. It was just moments and he could pick out what looked like seven, maybe eight riders coming on hard. *Hope this is Sloan and his men,* Slim thought, watching the group.

It was a short time and Slim recognized Charlie Sloan, then Pete Quimby, and signaled the group. "Lots of trouble in town," Slim said as Quimby brought his horse to a stop. "Sheriff shot old Tyler and Tater, and it looks like Holiday and the sheriff are going to try and kill Mrs. Flannigan and Cortez.

"I rode out to bring Sloan and his cowboys to town for help. Sure glad to see all of you." Slim was speaking so fast, was so excited that Quimby almost didn't understand. As if on cue, the group spurred their horses into a long lope and headed on toward the town.

Quimby and Red Feather, side by side, rode in silence with Sloan, Slim, young Pitts, and the Sloan cowboys strung out behind, kicking up a cloud of dust.

Sheridan George left his office and walked toward Holiday's saloon to tell him his plan to force the Flannigan woman to come to the aid of Tyler had backfired when Rose Flannigan and Reynaldo Cortez stepped out the hotel's front door.

"Get back inside, quick now," Cortez said to Rose, shoving her toward the door. George had his hand moving toward his sidearm but Cortez was faster. "Don't do it," Cortez snapped, his revolver out and aimed at the sheriff's chest. The two stood about fifteen feet apart, glaring at each other, waiting for the next move.

"I got no fight with you," George said, turning and walking off toward the Hearts of Gold Saloon, taking the big cowboy by complete surprise. Cortez wasn't the type of man to shoot someone in the back and just stood on the boardwalk watching the sheriff walk toward the saloon.

"Strangest thing I've ever seen," Reynaldo said to Rose when he stepped into the Red Rose Saloon. "Man just turned and walked away." He drank from a schooner of beer, wiped his hand across a large drooping moustache, and shook his head.

"If you look close, Rey, at the front windows of the saloon, you might understand," and she waved her arm toward the front of the large room where ten men with rifles and shotguns were standing, looking out the windows.

"And I thought the man was just scared of me," he joshed, taking another swig of cold beer. "He would have shot you, Rose. We have to do everything we can to keep you safe until Quimby and Sloan get here."

"These Peterson hands will do a fine job, Rey. What do you think Holiday's next move is going to be?"

"He knows Quimby is coming, and bringing help, and he knows we have sent riders to Sloan's ranch. He needs help now, and that would mean a hostage, I think. The obvious hostage would be you, and that's why these men are primed," he said, looking out across the saloon toward the windows.

***

"Your plan is worthless, Thorny. You might think you own a bank, you might think you own a couple of run-down ranches with some desert worn cattle, but what you do own, for sure, is trouble. That saloon down there is filled with cowboys, rifles, shotguns, and no fear. They aren't afraid of me, they aren't afraid of you."

Sheridan George was as angry as Holiday had ever seen him. "I've killed lots of men, Thorny, looked them in the eye and killed them, but I was just chased off by half a dozen cowboys with big guns."

"You're a coward, Sheridan. You were hired to make my plan work. I'm not going to be denied. This is my territory, and you were hired to protect it." Holiday's eyes were wild, he was screaming at the outlaw/sheriff. Those in the saloon just stood in place, no one moved. It was as if another person had been gunned down. "This is my territory, this is all mine, and you are supposed to be protecting this kingdom," Holiday screamed, getting right in George's face.

"You're mad, Thorny," George said, stepping back a foot or two. "You're insane," he said, not taking his eyes away from those of Holiday. Holiday's eyes were darting all over the saloon, glazed, wide, and not seeming to focus on anything. He turned, abruptly, and started toward the stairs leading to his second floor office. "No, Holiday," George thundered. "You're not walking away from this. Your plan has failed, you have failed, and you're not walking away, leaving this mess for me to clean up."

Holiday stopped about half way up the stairs, stood very still for a moment, turned and looked straight at Sheridan George. "You failed me, Sheridan. You're a coward and you failed me." He stood stock still for just one second and went for his revolver, much too slowly. The two bullets went through his heart before he cleared leather, and with eyes flashing madly about, he tumbled down the stairway, dead.

George looked around the barroom filled with the stunned former Holiday employees and hangers-on, no one making a move of any kind. "He was insane," George said, slipping the big forty-five back in its holster. "The only way any of us is getting out of here alive is for us to work together. Anyone want out, right this minute, go while you can. I won't stop you. But if you stay, you will do as I say with no questions asked."

He walked up to the bar and motioned for a bottle and glass, poured the glass full and drank half of it in one swallow. "Middleton is dead, Cooper is dead, and Colter is dead. Our only chance to get out of this alive is to hold a hostage, or if possible, more than one. I'm open to suggestions."

***

"We're about half an hour out, Red Feather," Quimby said, as they rode at a trot along the main trail into town. "Let's hold up and give the horses a breather and discuss how best to proceed once we hit town." He motioned for the riders to hold up and everyone stopped and dismounted. "Josh, how about you and one of you cowboys holding the horses while we talk for a spell."

"You said it would be best if we just rode in, but I wonder about that, Red Feather. We could be picked off as soon as we cleared Pitts's stables." The men were on their haunches along the side of the trail, some using the moment to drink from their canteens, some rolling a smoke, most worrying about the coming battle.

"Things have changed some since I said that, Pete," Red Feather said, "and I have your same worries. Is it possible for us to break up into groups of say, three or four, and ride in from different directions? Maybe even some of us able to sneak in unseen?" He cut a piece of dried meat and started chewing on it. "I remember you mentioning that there were at least three trails leading out of town."

"The Santa Fé road comes in from the east and continues out of town toward the west, and then this trail leads to Sloan's ranch heading north, with branches to other ranches, and there are two trails leading out toward the south, a main trail toward Mexico and a lesser trail to a couple of ranches." He was drawing this in the dust as he talked, with everyone trying to get a good view.

"I think we could have two or three coming in on the north-south trails and two or three coming in on the east-west trails. Charlie, you could take some men, have two or three come in from the west, and continue around

129

and have two or three come in from the south."

"No problem with that, Pete. Everyone here knows this country inside and out. I'll take four men, have two come in from the west, and me and two others will come in from the south," he said, standing and moving toward the horses, calling some names as he went.

Josh piped up right away. "Me and a couple of men can come in on the Santa Fé road. That's easy to get to from here."

"Holiday will be expecting riders coming in from Santa Fé, Josh. Take two men and circle around past that main road and come in on one of the ranch trails. They won't be expecting that. And Red Feather, you and I along with whoever is left, will come in on this trail.

"Any questions?"

"Not a question," Red Feather said, "just a thought. We can't all get there at the same time, so we will be on our own. Once you know you're getting close to town, be as careful and defensive as you can be. These men are all known killers and they won't think twice about shooting you.

"I've always believed in shooting first and being accurate. If you hesitate, you will die, so be ready at every instance, every moment."

They gathered their mounts and in little groups drifted off in scattered dust. "Pitts is awfully young to be getting into this kind of situation, Pete," Red Feather said as they stepped into their saddles. "I'd sure hate to have to tell his father he didn't make it."

"That boy's got more grit than half the town," Quimby said. "He knows fear and danger, and I'd rather have him back me up than his own father. Bill Pitts is a fine man, don't get me wrong, but his is the type to hesitate, to question what action to take, and as you just said, that will get you killed every time."

Quimby and Red Feather had two of Sloan's

cowboys with them as they moved back onto the trail. Slim rode with Josh and one other man. "I don't know what kind of mess we will be riding into," Quimby said to the two, "so just be prepared for anything." He turned to Red Feather, moving their horses into a fast walk. "I'm worried about Rose. Holiday knows she is alone, and she would make the perfect hostage if things get completely out of control."

"Put those kinds of thoughts aside, Pete," the big Indian said. "If you're worried about her and not paying attention to what's going on around you, you won't win. We're going to win this battle, Pete, just keep that in your mind."

Chapter Fourteen

S lim rode up alongside Josh Pitts, giving the boy a real look-see. "How old are you, Josh?" he asked. He was afraid the boy was too young to be in a mess like they would be riding into. "Do you know how dangerous this is?"

"Yes, I do," Josh answered right away. "I'm fourteen, Mr. Owens, and I work like a man. I'm probably just as afraid as you are, but I know what those outlaws in town have done, and I'm ready to fight them." He had a hard look on his face, Slim noted, and determination in his eyes. "I work side by side with Pa at the livery and we're starting up a lumber mill and I'll be doing a lot of that work. I'm a man, Mr. Owens," he said.

"I believe you, Josh," Slim said with a smile. Slim was remembering when he was fourteen, now twenty years ago. He worked on a big Texas spread after his mother and father were killed by rustlers. *Those thieves rode right up to our ranch house and shot my pa, then kidnapped Ma and we found her body a week later. The county people took the ranch, said a boy couldn't own a ranch. They were as big a thieves as the rustlers.*

Slim kept looking over at Josh as they rode cross country toward the Santa Fé road, kept remembering how things were, how he had been run off the ranch and almost starved before that one cowboy from Kansas had found him and took him in. *Just call me Kruger, he said,* Slim could almost picture the tall, skinny kid that found him holed up under some rocks, near Indian Territory, north of Texas.

Kruger was just a few years older than me, he remembered, *and taught me so much about horses, cattle, and mostly, men. After five years riding with Kruger, I could rightfully call myself a horseman, and I could look a rancher in the eye and say, 'yes, sir, I know cattle.' Died fightin' the Mexicans,* he remembered sadly.

Slim Owens learned fast the art and hard work of running cattle in open country, moving great herds north to the rail heads, of breeding and raising the young ones, and he learned something else, something he thought he could see in Josh Pitts' eyes. That of being a man with an honest soul. *He's still a boy,* Slim thought to himself, *and he's about to be tested. He's seen people he knows and cares about killed, he knows his way of life is being threatened, and now, he's in a position to do something about it. It's possible that the whole rest of his life will be determined by the choices he makes in the next day or two.*

"You know how to find that ranch trail Quimby was talking about?" Slim asked as they crossed the Santa Fé road, the one that continues for many miles both east and west.

"Yes, sir, I do," Josh said, and they put their horses into a nice trot, moving through the brush and desert, cross country to the ranch trail. "It's a couple of hours ahead of us. See those high mountains a little bit off to our right?" he asked, pointing mostly south of their position. "We'll pick up that trail a mile or so from them." Josh had a set to his jaw and rode his horse like he had been born in the saddle.

"You ride well, Josh. You ever worked with a young horse?"

"When I was twelve there was a man came to Plainsville from California. He was Mexican and wore some pretty fancy clothes. Pa called him a Vaquero, a man who rode and trained horses in a Spanish manner. Carlos Montoya was hired by Pa to work with half a dozen of our young colts and fillies, and he taught me everything I know about horses."

"He taught you well, my friend. He taught you well."

"He brought a two-year-old that had never even had a halter on him into the round pen one day and just stood there, didn't move, didn't talk to the horse, just stood there ignoring this big bad stud. I never seen anything like it, Mr. Owens, about two hours later that horse couldn't handle any more of being ignored, and just walked right up to Montoya and stood, looking at him.

"Montoya turned and walked away from that horse, and within a minute, that horse was right alongside him. He rubbed the horse all over with his hands after letting the horse smell him good, then just like that, slipped the halter on him and led him back to his stall.

"Mr. Owens, I'm not kidding," Josh was excited by being able to relive this wonderful moment in time, "Montoya was riding that horse within a week, and it never bucked once." Josh Pitts face was lit up like a gas lamp on a dark night telling the story. "This is him, Mr. Owens," he said, pointing at the horse's head that the boy was riding. "This is that horse, and he ain't never bucked one time."

"You have the touch, Josh," Slim said, watching as Josh and horse moved through the open country. "If they're still alive, or if I am able to find them, I've been breeding some fine Morgan horses for cattle work, Josh, and when all this is over, I'd be pleased if you would take over as trainer."

"I'm a partner with my pa in the new timber mill, and the blacksmith shop, and the livery stables, Mr. Owens. I sure would like to do that, but I don't think I could. Oh, my heavens," he said, "I sure would like to do that."

Slim smiled, thinking that sure as hell, Josh would be doing that.

***

Sheridan George filled and emptied his whiskey glass two more times, staring at the back bar, trying to work up a way to get out of this town, out of this mess, alive and with some of the gold in the bank. *Mad as a hen with power, and now what,* he was thinking. *How the hell am I getting out of this? Holiday has to have money stashed in that office upstairs, and the bank has more than I can carry, but I have to do this without any of these other bastards knowing what I'm doing, and without those town fools shooting my butt off.*

"We need a hostage," he said, turning from the bar. "Somebody those yokels will feel a desperate need to save," and he laughed along with many of the others, spread around the large saloon. "We ain't gonna get anywhere near that redheaded woman, so who has an idea? Come on, you gonna just sit and wait to die. Say something," he snarled, resting his hand on the revolver's handle, glaring at many of the men.

One of the men sitting at the faro table, John Horner, a former dealer down from the Dakotas, said, "How about that little hotel clerk? Rose Flannigan sure takes good care of him."

"You're on," George snapped. "Your idea, you go get him. Bring him upstairs to the office." He turned to go up to the office, stopped, and said, "You get him, bring him to me, and it's a hundred dollars for you. Take somebody with you." He took the stairs two at a time, and went into Holiday's office.

"First, ex-King Holiday," he growled, "some of your sippin' whiskey." He poured a full glass and drank half of it down in one gulp, letting a smile spill across his face. "Sip this, your majesty," he quipped, and drank the second half, pouring another before starting his search for gold and money.

Horner and Thomas 'Knife' Windsor headed out the back door of the saloon. "They's a carriage house behind the hotel and we might be able to sneak in the back way and grab that little guy." He smiled over to Windsor. "Don't worry, I'll split that hundred with you, if George actually comes through. Can't trust that man." Windsor gave him a sardonic smile back, thinking, *You damn right I get half.*

"Looked like they had most of the town tucked up

in the Red Rose Saloon, so this should be quick and quiet,"
Horner said, leading the way. They circled out and away
from the buildings, trying to stay in the mid-day shadows,
reaching the carriage house quickly.

"Looks like somebody inside the hotel door there,
Horner," Knife said as they crept closer. "What are we
gonna do now?" he asked, down on his haunches, watching
the scene through tall grass.

Horner leaned back against the carriage house,
thinking, finally saying, "You sneak up as close to that door
as possible, off to the side that it opens from, and I'll make
some noise. Maybe that guard will come out to check and
you take him down."

Windsor pulled a long stiletto type knife from a belt
sheath, the blade glinting and mean-sharp, waiting for the
taste of blood. He moved low and slow to the door,
pressing as close as possible to the side of the hotel
building, while Horner slipped into the carriage house.
Horner found some wooden boxes piled up near the double
doors. He opened the double doors just a few inches, then
toppled the boxes, letting them tumble through the doors,
spilling onto the ground between the carriage house and the
hotel.

As expected, the man inside came out through the
back door of the hotel at a run, finding a long thin blade
shoved between his shoulder blades before he got two steps
out. Windsor stabbed him twice more, just to be sure, and
the two men slipped into the hallway at the back of the
hotel, running into Gerald Sorenson, coming out of Rose
Flannigan's office.

Horner slammed the little clerk across the side of
the head with his revolver and threw him over his shoulder.
The two outlaws ran back to the Hearts of Gold Saloon
with their hostage, whooping and hollering coming in the
back door. No one at the Plainsville hotel was the wiser.

Sheridan George heard the commotion downstairs

but was too busy counting twenty-dollar gold coins to be bothered. "How the hell did that man get this much money?" he muttered, reaching deep into five figures and still counting. "How the hell did he carry it?" The chorus of howls continued downstairs and George finally had to quit and find out what was going on. He stashed the gold back into the three large canvas bags and tucked them into a safe before leaving the office.

Horner met him on the landing outside the office. "We got him, George, we got him," and led the big man downstairs. Sorenson was sitting at a cocktail table, bleeding heavily from his head wound, and groggy as well. Two men were busy wrapping rope around the man, now tied securely to the chair.

"Good work, Horner. Let's get him over by the windows so he can be seen."

"Let's not forget the hundred dollars, George," Horner said.

"You'll get it, just like I said," Sheridan George said. Actually, George's mind wasn't on Gerald Sorenson, it was on three large bags of gold upstairs. *How the hell am I going to get that out of here?* He kept saying to himself, watching four men carry the hotel clerk across the saloon, tied up to a chair. *I'm going to have to have help, and that means sharing some of it. Damn you, Holiday,* he almost muttered out loud.

***

"Where's Gerald?" Rose Flannigan asked as Reynaldo Cortez walked up to the bar, holding a large pot of coffee from the café. "I sent him back to the office half an hour ago, Rey. Did you see him?"

"No," Cortez answered. "Jaime Juarez is at the back door. Maybe they're talking. I'll go back and check. Here's some fresh coffee and Rosie is sending over food in an hour or so. Be right back," and he motioned for one of the Peterson cowboys to go with him.

Half way down the corridor Cortez spotted the back door swinging in the wind. "Something's wrong," he said to the cowboy. "Go get help, and hurry." Cortez had his weapon in hand and slowly crept down the hallway, past the baths and dentist, and past Rose Flannigan's office door, which stood open as well.

It was just moments and three armed men rushed down the corridor toward the open door. Cortez was standing in the weeds just outside the doorway, looking at the body of the Peterson cowboy. "It looks like Gerald Sorenson is probably either very dead or a hostage," Reynaldo said to the group. "Let's go back. Rose won't like this."

Chapter Fifteen

C harlie Sloan had his horse in a solid trot, knew it would still be an hour or more before they were in Plainsville, and angry that what was taking place today should have taken place weeks ago. "I like Quimby," he said to the man riding alongside him, "but he is too set on following the letter of the law. What galls me, there is no law out here. I should have gathered all the hands from the ranches and just run that Holiday gang right out of town."

His mouth was grim, his eyes narrowed, and his free hand was balled in a fist that could break a man's jaw with ease. "Morton and Peterson, simply murdered, and what are we doing? Exactly what I suggested weeks ago."

"You're right boss, except for one thing. Quimby and that other feller are wearing badges, and that changes our name from vigilante to posse."

"See?" Sloan exploded. "That's what I mean. It was just a name change, and in the meantime, good people died. Well, I'm telling you right now, bad people are gonna die when I get to town." He sat straight in the saddle, harrumphed a couple more times, glared at the desert, glared at his riding partner, and kicked his cow pony up a notch, into a nice long lope.

Sloan came to New Mexico Territory following the war that created the new frontier, from Texas where he bossed several large cattle operations. In those earlier times, the ranch made the rules, saw to it the rules were followed, and found little reason to ever ask for help from something like a government. There was considerable lawlessness in those times, which led to the formation of the Texas Rangers, and eventually even the largest of the cattle barons allowed as how maybe the government law dogs should make the decisions on how rules should be followed.

If Charlie Sloan were to be asked, he would probably scoff at the whole idea. "Man tries to steal my cattle, man dies," is something that might be said, or, "I built this ranch, raised these animals, and I see to it that things are run right." Sloan always looked up to Pete Quimby, but considered his ideas on how to take care of the Holiday gang wrong.

"Let's start making that swing more toward the town. Should cross the main trail just ahead there, and then we can ease the horses back some," he said to his companions. "Sure wish there was some way for us to know where the other groups are," he said, thinking it would not be a good thing to ride into that nest of outlaws with just three people. "What do you think, Shorty?"

Shorty Flint was Sloan's cow boss, a cow and horseman from the old school who saw to it that Sloan's herd was one of the finest in the territory and whose remuda ranked among the best as well. Shorty stands almost six feet and three inches and when he's sideways to you, you could lose sight of him. His mother gave him the name, in jest.

"Think we'd do well to ride in quiet like and tie off right away. I imagine old Reynaldo has everyone holed up at the Red Rose, so we probably should join them."

"That's pretty much what I was thinking," Sloan said. "I wonder if Pitts has some people with him at the livery. This is gonna be damn dangerous, Shorty. Those men are gonna be set up in a fortress, and we could have snuffed this whole thing out weeks ago." His anger was not going to cool down.

***

"Sure wish there was some way we could know when the other groups are going to be coming into town," Pete Quimby said, as he and Red Feather were breaking trail through brush and desert. "I guess just move in slow and quiet, and try to make contact with Rose and whoever is still in town alive."

Quimby knew that town's layout better than anyone and was working on how to best get into town without getting shot-up. "Think we ought to come in somewhere near my corrals," he said. "We can stay out of sight but still see most of the town. We need that advantage," he smiled, watching Red Feather nod in agreement.

Quimby had Rose Flannigan on his mind all morning, and during this ride. "She's a strong lady, Red Feather, and a born leader. When you meet her, just watch out for that temper," and he had to laugh, thinking about how she would explode sometimes. "She has been known to throw heavy objects, has a strong and accurate arm, too."

"I'm looking forward to meeting her, Pete. It's a shame this had to reach this point with Holiday and his gang, but I think we will come out fine. Like you said, if we ride in slow and quiet, get the horses taken care of, we can then organize and figure out how to take care of that nest of outlaws. They need to know who we are, what our authority is, and be aware that they can't win." He almost snickered, saying, "Not too big an order, is it?"

Red Feather got contemplative for a few minutes as they moved from brush busting onto the western arm of the main road. "I think this Holiday fellow might just be suffering from a self-inflated ego, thinking he is a European land baron, or maybe like some of those Spanish Land Grantees. Conclaves of self-rule established by men who have very high opinions of themselves.

"That makes Holiday a very dangerous person. In a word, he is out of his mind, insane with power, and jealous of his status. He thinks his word is law, he makes all the decisions, and he has no morals. If he wants something, he takes it. I think that is what he's set up, using the bank and his phony sheriff to do all the dirty work. He has probably promised them a piece of the action, and has no plans to let them have any."

They rode quietly for the next many miles, wondering exactly what they would find when they arrived. *A beautiful little town settled by good people in a valley surrounded by large ranches,* Quimby was thinking, seeing the great expanse of the valley, hills, blue gray in the distance, towering spring clouds moving through a pale blue sky. *Those bastards are not going to get away with this. That railroad is going to be built, Plainsville will be a real town, with real laws and elected leaders. Fifty years ago, Charlie Sloan would have been considered right, vigilante justice might have been the only way, but not today. In these times, law is the right way, justice by way of law, is the way our community will grow and prosper.* Quimby spent many long minutes putting the town of Plainsville together in his mind, built and re-built his stockyards, helped the railroad people get their rails into the town, and wondered, for the first time, why Plainsville had not done any of these things before.

Didn't have to, he realized. *We didn't have any incentive to build a town, create a local government. We weren't threatened by anyone or anything. Too damn comfortable and Holiday saw that.* He was angry with himself, knowing he was also one of the town's leading figures. *I'm as responsible for what's happening as Holiday,* he snarled to himself.

***

"Riders," Red Feather said, and Quimby came out of his reverie immediately. "Four of 'em, heading out fast. Let's get in the brush, in this gully," and they rode through heavy sage and greasewood into a shallow arroyo, watching the riders come toward them at a full gallop.

"They're heading for Peterson's," Quimby said. Probably going to get help from those left at the Peterson ranch."

"Not this time, they're not," Red Feather said, stepping off his horse, bringing his carbine with him. "You take the two trailing, I'll take the two leaders," he said, kneeling in the brush, jacking a round into the chamber.

Quimby dismounted with his big Henry and followed Red Feather into a kneeling position. "Let them get close," he whispered, putting his rifle to his shoulder, watching the sights slowly descend onto a rider's chest, and squeezed off a round. He jacked the second round in, and dropped number two.

Red Feather took out the leading riders, and they walked up to the trail with their horses. "Know any of these jaspers?" he asked, rolling one onto his back.

Quimby shook his head, giving each a good look. "Nope," he said, "but it does help with the odds when we get into town. Wonder why four men would ride out if they were going for help? It wouldn't take four men to get help."

"The mind of a criminal is something that can't be understood by those that aren't criminals, and with Holiday, a criminal most of his life, a mind warped by self love. Did he send these four men out for some mission? Or, Pete Quimby, are they running away from a coming disaster? We'll probably never know," he said with a wry smile splashed across his face.

They remounted after moving the bodies off the trail, each trailing two horses as they rode toward town.

***

Several of the men in the Red Rose Saloon saw Gerald Swanson being marched out of the Hearts of Gold Saloon and called to Rose Flannigan and Reynaldo Cortez. "Looks like they want to pow-wow some," one of the cowboys said. "Got that hotel clerk trussed up like a pig on a spit, and the sheriff is standing behind him with his gun pointed at his head."

"Don't get too close to those windows," Cortez admonished Rose, as they moved quickly to see what was happening. "They have men with rifles in there."

Sorenson appeared to be unconscious, held up by a

man on each side with George behind him holding the revolver. Cortez walked out the doors of the saloon, staying behind one of the porch supports, and called to George. "You might live through this, George, if you let that man go."

"He'll be alive if you let us ride out of town, peaceful like," Sheridan George yelled back.

He was interrupted by the sound of horses galloping away from the back of the Hearts of Gold Saloon. Everyone watched four riders make for the Santa Fé road, and George screaming at them. He fired several shots from his handgun, but they were well out of range. "You bastard cowards," he screamed, over and over, then slammed Sorenson across the side of the head with his gun, and the group dashed back into the saloon.

"Oh, God, poor Gerald," Rose said, flushed with anger and sorrow. "They'll kill him, won't they," she said, softly to Reynaldo, gripping his arm when he came back inside the saloon. "Hold me close, Rey. He's been with me since I got here, never hurt anyone. I've never heard him speak an unkind word about anyone. Damn," she said, as she squeezed his arm hard enough to bring a bruise. Her eyes filled with tears, as sad as anything Reynaldo Cortez had ever seen. She just kept squeezing his arm, kept looking deep into his eyes.

"He's going to die, isn't he?" she sobbed.

"I'm afraid so, Rose. Looks like Holiday's gang is breaking up. Strange," he said, almost thinking out-loud, "it was George with the hostage, not Holiday. I wonder if that shot we heard earlier was the end of King Holiday?" *I've never seen such sad eyes. The strongest woman I've ever known, and so filled with emotion. I wonder why she isn't married, why she doesn't have six or seven little ones hanging onto her skirts.* It was the danger of the situation that broke his reverie.

He motioned for everyone to get back from the

window and open door, and helped Rose settle into a chair at one of the tables. He joined her. *We're both too old to have children,* he was thinking, *but I'd give up my cowboy life to spend the rest of mine with her.*

"Pete and whoever he's bringing with him should be arriving very soon, Rose, and Slim should have found Charlie Sloan by now, and hopefully will be bringing them into town. Keep your chin up. The next several hours won't be nice, but you're strong. You'll be ok."

"Don't you worry about me," Rose said, anger flashing in those Irish eyes. She reached across the table and took his hand, giving a good squeeze, letting her anger calm down, smiling gently to the big cowman. "Right now, Sheridan George needs to worry about me, so does that phony banker Swanson, and most of all, that bastard Thornton Holiday.

"Do we have to wait for Pete? Why don't we attack?" she scowled. "Why don't we kill those fools, take our town back, make them suffer and hurt?" Cortez sat very quiet, letting her vent, letting the rage burn, and the anger flush. *This is the strongest woman I've ever met,* he said to himself, again, still holding her hand, looking deep into blazing eyes. Some of the cowboys along with Old Pete stayed at the far end of the bar.

"We have the people, Rey," she said, quietly. "We don't have to sit here like victims, like little children sent to their room. We should make an effort to fight those horrible men."

Reynaldo Cortez had never met a woman quite like Rose Flannigan, and sat for a moment, deep in thought. *She isn't the least bit wrong,* he thought. *We could send small groups of two or three to harass the hell out them.* "Rose," he finally said, "I think you may just be right." He stood up, smiled down into her face, and motioned the men to gather around the table.

"I think we need to organize a few little groups and

145

see what kind of problems we can create for Mr. Holiday and his gang. Who wants to try to get yourself to the livery and do some serious rifle damage?" Several hands went up and Cortez picked two. "Try not to be seen getting over there. Bill Pitts should be there, and just make those people in the saloon suffer some." There was almost a round of hurrahs following that, and Cortez kept it going with two more men sent to create problems at the back of the saloon.

"That's where Holiday has his well. Take a position near that well and anyone coming for water, kill 'em. Anyone coming out of that saloon, kill 'em." Cortez put another man at the back of the hotel, so there would be two guarding that door.

"Thank you, Rey, that makes me feel better. Pete, let's put the coffee aside and have a round of cold beer to get this war started." This time, there really was cheering.

***

It was very quiet in the Hearts of Gold Saloon, only the sound of Sheridan George's boots as he stormed about the large room, dragging the still unconscious Gerald Sorenson around by the ropes he was tied with. He flung the small man at one of the Holiday thugs and walked briskly up the stairs to Holiday's office, his language as foul as any of the men had heard.

Inside, he poured a glass of whiskey and sat at Holiday's desk, drumming his fingers, still cursing loudly. "I have to get out of town, and this gold has to go with me," he said, smashing a balled up fist into the desk. "I told that son of a bitch, we don't build banks, we rob them. We don't run cattle ranches, we rustle cattle. Now, look what the hell we're in. Should have killed the insane bastard as soon as I heard his fool plan." He tried to let his mind calm down, tried to think, and was mired in useless thought. "I can't carry this much gold," he said to the room, "and I'm not giving one coin up."

The idea that he had three bags filled with gold

146

coins because of Holiday's insane plan never entered the liquor sotted mind of Sheridan George. George couldn't understand that if Holiday had simply followed the law, minus the killings, those bags would still be filled, and there would be no crisis. Criminals are not deep thinkers.

He poured another glass of whiskey, got up from the desk and paced about the room, cursing, spitting, kicking furniture, and sat back down. "I have to hide the gold," he said, pouring another glass, not feeling the effects of all that liquor at all. "Where will I hide it," he wondered, "and how will I get it there?"

Noise from downstairs interrupted his thoughts and he walked to the head of the stairs, watching several men fighting. "What's going on?" he howled, coming down the stairs two at a time.

"Terry found Chuck trying to sneak out, and they're goin' at it," one of the outlaws said.

Chuck was bleeding from a cut lip and broken nose. "That true, Chuck? You runnin' out on me?" Chuck didn't answer, just stood there, Terry next to him, ready to knock him around some more. He didn't get the chance as George drew his weapon and shot the man dead, one round through the heart.

"Coward," was all he said, waving the smoking revolver around. "Anyone else want to run out on me?" he snarled, glaring from one to another around the room. "If we don't stick together, we ain't gonna live," he spat, turned, and went back upstairs. "Get that body taken care of."

Holiday had done a fine job of making the town of Plainsville a haven for outlaws, and right now, Sheridan George had at least twenty men standing around in the saloon, each an independent outlaw, only there because of supposed protection from the now dead Holiday. There was no loyalty to George, probably just limited loyalty to the dead Holiday.

Holiday had offered land, a ranch, and protection to active outlaws, and many like Sheridan George, only wanted the spoils, the gold. George was right when he figured there was no loyalty toward him, and with Holiday dead, no loyalty toward anything but the spoils, the gold.

Everyone in the room had thoughts of stealing what they could from the saloon, maybe even the bank, and going on the run. The Hearts of Gold Saloon, despite being relatively new, was a very successful operation and more than one of the outlaws was aware of just how much money Holiday kept on hand, and how much was tucked away in that new bank of his.

Back at Holiday's desk, Sheridan George remembered what the men said when they brought the hotel clerk in, about the carriage house behind the hotel. *What was it?* he wondered, then remembered. *Looked like it hadn't been used in years, is what he said. If I keep those men busy I might be able to sneak most of this gold into that old building, get it hidden well, and come back for it later.*

He sat back in Holiday's chair, poured another glass of whiskey, and lit a cheroot. He chuckled to himself, smiled slightly, and took a healthy drink, working on a plan. *First, I gotta get these bags near that back door without being seen, then get them into the carriage house. I can do that part when the sun goes down, but getting them down to the back door will be the hard part.*

Terry and a couple of men grabbed the dead Chuck and dragged him toward the back of the saloon. "Just toss his worthless ass out the back door, I guess," Terry said. They tugged and pulled the heavy man down the long corridor behind the gambling area, leaving a trail of blood on the hardwood floor, and opened the back door. "Just shove him out into the weeds. Let him rot in the sun," he laughed, helping the men get him through the door. Two shots rang out, both ripping through the chest of Terry, flinging him around and into the ground face first.

The others dove through the open door, back into the building, not bothering to try and shut the door. They were at a full run as they sprinted into the main saloon gallery, George coming down the stairway, again. "What the hell, now?" he demanded, stopping about three steps from the bottom.

"Men out back with rifles," one of them said, out of breath. "Terry's dead." George muttered something obscene and walked back up to Holiday's office.

"New plan," he said, pouring another drink.

The two Peterson cowboys, hidden in the brush and weeds behind the Hearts of Gold Saloon congratulated themselves on killing one of the men. "Strange, they were dragging a dead man out the door," the man called "Worry" said. He got his name from always worrying about whatever it was they were supposed to be working on. "If any others come out, let's each take out one instead of us both shootin' the same one." He straightened up some, cocking his head to the side.

"Sounds like horses," he said, standing up. "Two or three, at least. Better let Reynaldo know," he said. "I'll stay here, watching that door. You hightail it inside and get some help out here."

Chapter Sixteen

S onny Bergstrom and Kirk Taylor left out of the Red Rose Saloon by way of the back door of the hotel and followed along behind the buildings for about three hundred feet, then went between the Emporium Building and the one next to it back to the main street, planning to cross the street, get to the block behind the sheriff's office, and work their way back toward the livery. "Won't take us ten minutes," Bergstrom said, leading the way.

They made a long circle, staying as close to buildings as they could, and used some large cottonwood trees near the livery to hide their dash across the roadway and into the main barn. They were stopped dead in their track by Bill Pitts holding a double barrel shotgun, pointed and cocked.

"One more step and you both die," he snarled, legs spread slightly, ready to absorb the blunt force of both barrels going off at the same time.

"We're with Mrs. Flannigan and Reynaldo Cortez," Bergstrom said, pulling up to a halt, his heart pounding, staring down the barrels of Pitts's big gun. Both he and Taylor had their arms spread wide, as far away from their holsters as possible. "They want us to use the livery to be able to shoot into the saloon where Holiday's gang is." He was talking as fast as he could, expecting those monster barrels to fill with fire and lead shot at any moment. "We worked for Peterson. Cortez sent us."

Pitts stood silent for a minute, then slowly let the big gun come down off his shoulder. A slight smile came across his face and he ushered the two into his office. "Heard lots of activity at Holiday's place, even saw that vile Sheridan George holding Gerald Sorenson hostage. You boys know what's going on?"

"'Bout the same as you," Taylor said. "Heard

shootin' goin' on over there," he said, jerking his head toward the gaudy saloon, "but don't know what it means." Taylor was a rangy Texas cowboy, long and lean with large hands gnarled from years throwing ropes, branding calves, and shoeing horses. He set his rifle down to roll a cigarette, looking around the office, in particular a window facing at an angle toward the Holiday saloon.

"You heard anything from Charlie Sloan or big Pete Quimby? We ain't heard nothin' over there," he said, putting a hot coal to his smoke.

Pitts offered boiling mugs of coffee and sat down at his desk. "Been expecting them all day," he said, shaking his head. "Should have been here a couple of hours ago, is what I've been thinking."

Bergstrom had moved to the open window, looking out across the plaza toward the Holiday saloon, brought his rifle up, taking a long slow aim. He fired once, jacked a round into the chamber and fired once more. "There's one less fool we gots to deal with," he muttered, reloading the rifle.

"Guess old Reynaldo knew what he was talking about, eh, Taylor?" he said with a smile. "That old boy was just standing at the side of the doors, pretty as a big buck deer, not paying any attention to anything. Bet none of those other fools will, though," he said, coming back for a taste of coffee.

Pitts stood up fast and walked to the door. "You just hear a horse nicker?" he asked. All three men moved into the barn and near the open doors, craning their heads out as far as they dared, listening for the slightest sound.

"There," Taylor said. "Over by the stockyards. There," and he pointed at three riders coming in, slow and quiet. "That's Quimby," he said, pointing at a large man on a tall horse, moving slowly through and around the various pens at the stockyards. They watched as the three riders dismounted, and moved toward the main street.

Pitts put his hat on top of that long shotgun and started waving it back and forth. Quimby and Red Feather spotted it immediately. "That's Bill Pitts," Quimby said, pointing out the waving hat. "I think he wants us to come to the livery instead of the hotel." He looked at the Sloan cowboy that was with them. "You stay here with Red Feather and I'll go check on what Pitts is up to." He started toward the livery, then stopped for a minute.

"Keep an eye on me, Red Feather. Neither you nor Pancake can go to the hotel. They'll shoot you, so wait for me to either come back or call you to join me," and he headed off, low and slow toward the livery. *Pitts didn't come out of the barn to holler at me and didn't signal from outside either. Tells me something is already happening around this old burg. Hope to hell Rose is ok.* He tried to quell the anxious thoughts, clear his mind for the job at hand, getting to the livery without being seen by whoever might be in the Hearts of Gold Saloon.

***

Worry burrowed himself back into some bushes behind the Hearts of Gold Saloon, listening for either horse sounds or man sounds, and he didn't have long to wait. Two horses, walking slow, came down the old ranch trail leading into town, and Worry crawled on his belly further into the weeds, trying to get a good look.

"We better hold up here," Josh Pitts said as the large saloon building came into view. "We can get to the Red Rose or the hotel on foot without being seen." He and Slim dismounted just in time to find Worry coming out of the bushes.

"Sure glad to see you two," he said, motioning them to follow him as he turned to snake back into the weeds. "Things are starting to get hot," he whispered, moving quickly toward the back of the hotel. "Everybody's really worried about whether anyone was gonna show up to help."

"We're here, Worry. You can relax," Slim

152

chuckled, watching Reynaldo Cortez standing at the back door of the saloon. The three got to their feet and sprinted the last few yards and into the building.

"Welcome home, boys," Reynaldo said, holding the door open. "Sure glad to see you. Where's the rest? You're not alone, are you? Where's Quimby and Sloan?"

"They're coming," Slim said, catching his breath. "I'll tell you all about it, soon as I get a cold beer to wash out all this trail dust."

"Me too," Josh said, and the men all said, no at the same time.

***

"You have any idea where we are, boss?" one of the riders said as they moved slowly through some heavy sage and other brush, walking their horses slow.

"When we top that little ridge in front of us, we'll be looking right down the main street of Plainsville," Charlie Sloan said, spitting a wad of juice into the dust. "I don't think we want to ride over that ridge. Let's tie off back here, get well off to the side of the road, and sneak in quiet like."

The three cowboys and Sloan moved slow as they topped the ridge and looked into town. They were about two hundred yards from the nearest building, which was about two blocks south of the Plainsville Hotel. "We'll move up to the side of that first building, then move real slow down the street. Don't want to be seen by any of that Holiday crowd."

Charlie led them down the slope of the ridge and up to the first building. "The next building is that new bank, and remember, the Sheriff's office is real close." They snuck around the corner, edging their way toward the bank building and spotted Henry Swanson standing in the open doorway.

Sloan leaped toward Swanson just as Swanson spotted him and the other cowboys, knocking the banker into the building. The other three came right in as well, closing the door after them. "You ain't goin' nowhere," Sloan snarled, crushing the banker's nose with his big right fist. "Sit your pukin' ass down," he said, shoving the banker into one of the chairs in his large, rather over-done office.

"You got some explaining to do, Swanson, and I'm ready to do the listening." He sat on the edge of a massive oak and marble desk, letting his free hand, the one not holding a rifle, fondle the handle of his revolver. "You boys keep an eye on the street while the banker and I have a nice friendly conversation."

"I don't see nothin' goin' on at the Red Rose Saloon," one of the cowboys said, but there are four or five men standing in the open doors at the livery. One of 'em's Quimby for sure, and I think Bill Pitts."

"Good," Charlie Sloan said. "That end of town's taken care of, and it's up to us to make this end of town peaceable. Ain't that right, banker?" he said, slapping the man hard, and glaring into his eyes. "This end of town ain't been took care of properly for some time, has it banker," and he slapped him again. His pent up rage was coming to the surface, week on week, he had wanted to take it to the Holiday gang, and he's using Swanson as his starting point.

Sloan walked around behind the desk and started opening one of the many drawers. Swanson yelled, "You get away from there. That's private. That's not for you to be looking at" and he started to get up, hearing the fast click of a hammer being cocked, ready to blow his head off.

"Sit down and shut up," Sloan barked, keeping the revolver aimed at the banker's nose. Swanson could see all the cylinders filled with lead, could see death in Charlie Sloan's face, and slumped back into his chair, hoping to hell that Sloan wouldn't find one of the blank loan applications with the false second page.

"Many of my friends are dead, banker. They died soon after taking a loan out at your bank. I took a loan out at your bank. Were you planning to have me killed also?" He opened the top drawer on the left side of the desk, rummaging around through several files, finding one saying, 'Applications.'

"Well now, lookie here," Sloan said, opening the ledger. He was paging through an empty loan application form when he stopped suddenly, and laid one down on the desk, reading word for word through the page. Swanson was fidgeting on his chair, and suddenly bolted for the front door of the bank, one of the cowboys swinging his rifle around like a club, knocked the man back into the office, unconscious and bleeding heavily.

"Thank you, Freddie," Sloan said, his weapon in hand. "You just saved that man's life. Remember to tell him how much he owes you," and he went back to reading the paper in front of him. It was when he turned to page two that the anger boiled over. "So, this is how they did it," he muttered, going back and forth between page one and page two. "Clever, I'll sure as hell give 'em that."

Sloan stood up and walked around from behind the desk. "Put this fool in a chair and find something to tie him up with. We need to keep him alive and well so we can watch him dance at the end of a rope and die nice and slow." He wanted to kick him in the head, empty his revolver into his head, then shoot him five times with his repeating rifle, but instead, just stood and stared angry thoughts at the man.

"See anything up at the livery?" he asked, finally walking away from the banker.

***

Black Sam Wadsworth was pacing back and forth in front of the long bar in the Hearts of Gold Saloon, cussing a blue streak when Jake Salerno finally told him to knock it off. "Go to hell, Salerno. What makes you the boss? What

155

the hell makes George the boss? Why should I even have a boss?" He paced some more, then turned to the rest of the outlaws, now gathered in little groups.

"That fool upstairs ain't the boss just cuz he killed Holiday," he said. "Who made him boss?" He continued his pacing. "He made himself boss and we just let him do it. He thinks all the gold Holiday had is his, now. All the whiskey behind the bar is his. The bank down the street is his.

"Well, Mister phony sheriff, it ain't. I say, it's ours," and he vaulted over the bar, grabbed a bottle of good whiskey, popped the cork, and took a long drink, almost coughing as he swallowed. "Damn good whiskey, this stuff of ours," he laughed, taking another drink.

A couple of the outlaws started to move toward the bar and Black Sam pulled a few bottles off the shelves and put them on the bar. "Here's what I think," Black Sam said. "I think we ought to go up them stairs and take that gold from Holiday's office and split it up, and then go down the street to that bank and take all the gold from there and split it up. That's what I think. And if that phony sheriff who thinks all this is his gets in the way, I think he's gonna die. That's what I think."

There was dead silence in the bar as most discovered that Sheridan George was standing about half way down the stairs, listening to every word Black Sam had said. He looked about the men and slowly, one long footstep at a time, came down the last few stairs onto the barroom floor. "That's what you think," he snarled, pulling his iron and fanning two quick shots, one exploding the bottle in Sam's hand, the other nailing the big man between the eyes.

He turned, smoking revolver in hand, cocked and ready for the next shot. "What do you think?" he asked, shoving the weapon under the chin of one of the outlaws. "Or you?" he asked, spinning and aiming at another.

156

"Holiday and I put this plan together and Holiday failed me and paid the penalty. Anybody else want to fail me?" He glared at the men, one at a time, that big piece of still hot iron threatening each one. "Ain't nobody gonna take this away from me, and if you're with me, if you don't fail me, there's gonna be plenty left over for everybody."

He turned and stalked back upstairs, stopping about half way up. "Get that stinking body out of here."

Two men pulled Black Sam's hulk from behind the bar and started dragging toward the back door. They got about half way down the hallway and stopped. "I ain't goin out that door," one of them said, dropping the arm he was holding. The other let go of Black Sam as well, and they returned to the main saloon. "Let him rot right there, for all I care," he said.

***

"It's been like that all day, Quimby. Every once in a while a shot or two," Pitts said as they sat down at his large table in the office. Bergstrom was standing near the open door of the livery and Taylor was back at the office window, both keeping an eye on the front of Holiday's saloon. Red Feather and the cowboy had been called in by Quimby and they were gathered as Pitts poured coffee all around and sat down.

"I saw movement toward the south end of town," Red Feather said. "I think Sloan and his riders are here. Hope your son, Josh and Slim have already got here too," he said, nodding to Bill Pitts. "That's quite a boy you have, and about the best horseman I've seen in a long time."

"I've never been more proud of him," Pitts choked, saying it. "You said Slim, from Peterson's spread, is with him?"

"They are supposed to come in from the northeast ranch road. Should already be here," Quimby answered. "What's our best move, now that we're here, Red Feather?"

"We have to establish who we are, Pete, then give

them the chance to surrender. We can't actually make a plan until they declare their intentions. I represent Territorial Law and you're my immediate deputy, representing Plainsville district. Holiday, George, and that banker must be made aware of that."

"What if they tell you to go to hell?" Pitts asked, taking a long drink of hot coffee.

"That's just about guaranteed, Mr. Pitts," Red Feather chuckled. "Pete, you and I need to get over to the Red Rose Saloon, Pitts you and these men need to continue keeping Holiday and company busy. Prepare to give us cover as we make our way to the stockyards, and then over to the saloon," he said, nodding at Quimby, and moving toward the large livery barn doors.

Chapter Seventeen

"Here comes Quimby," someone shouted from the saloon door as Red Feather and Pete Quimby sprinted across the street toward the saloon. One shot rang out from the Hearts of Gold Saloon, splashing dust between Quimby's feet, and it was answered by five rifle shots from the livery. The two men came through the swinging doors at a full gallop.

"About time you got here," Rose Flannigan said, a smile a mile wide splashed across her tired and worried face. She wanted to tell him everything that had been going on in Plainsville, wanted to hear everything from him, and all at the same time. All she said, was, "Thank God you're safe."

"Safe and angry," he said, giving her a good hug. "Meet my new boss," Quimby said with a smile. "This is Jose Red Feather, territorial law, and I'm his deputy for this area."

Rose stuck her hand out. "Nice to meet you, Red Feather. You'll have your work cut out keeping this big guy in line."

"I've heard nothing but good things about you, Mrs. Flannigan," the big man said with a smile. "Please, bring us up to date on what has happened and what is happening," he said, indicating they should sit at a table.

"I will," Rose said. She looked over to Reynaldo, saying, "Please join us, Rey. This is Reynaldo Cortez, he was foreman at the Peterson Ranch before Don was killed, and has been working overtime keeping all of us safe these last few days." She took Cortez's hand, and held it as they talked.

Quimby recognized the gesture, nodded to Cortez, then to Rose, almost as giving the pairing his blessing. "I see some things have changed around here," he smiled. "For the better, I do believe." His southern charm oozed across the table, making Rey Cortez blush a bit, bringing a smile to Rose Flannigan.

Reynaldo Cortez, shaking hands with Quimby and Red Feather, said, "I'm glad you're back safe, Pete. Most of the Holiday gang is holed up at the Hearts of Gold Saloon, but they also are holding Gerald Sorenson hostage, if he's even still alive. That fool Sheridan George says he'll give him up for safe passage out of town. We didn't even bother to answer."

"Good," said Red Feather. "Right now there are several people at the livery with Bill Pitts, and Charlie Sloan has more down near the bank. I have the feeling there is a tremendous amount of money involved here, and Holiday and George are not going to give it up easily. Do you know about how many men there are in that saloon? And does Holiday have more people coming in?"

"If we're counting right," Rose said, "we think there are probably around twenty men in there, along with a few of the working girls. There have been several shots fired inside, not at us, so that number might be slightly less. Do you have any kind of plan to root those foul people out of there, get our town back?"

"That's what we're going to put together right now," Pete said. "Did you say that Don Peterson is dead?"

"Yes," Cortez answered. "They killed him the same way they did Morton, and they tortured and killed Tater, the telegraph man. They tried to set up one of our cowboys, Tyler, but he gunned down Mike Middleton and one other George man, and then was killed by George. They have been on a rampage, Pete."

"That's about to end," Quimby said, his face knotted in anger. He spotted young Josh Pitts standing near the bar. "Josh," he yelled over. "Glad you made it through, son. Good work. Meet any bad guys?"

"Yes, but they won't be a problem any longer. We didn't meet anybody until we got to town. Nobody on the trail."

Pete nodded and smiled. "Good," he said. "Now, Red Feather and I have to make ourselves known as legitimate lawmen to Holiday and George, and depending on their response, we will make our plans. I'm pretty sure I know what their response is going to be, but that move has to be made first."

"Because of Tater, they know you and Red Feather are territorial lawmen," Rose said. "They beat it out of him before killing him. They also killed Don Jenkins, but he killed Cooper and wounded Middleton before being gunned down." She took a deep breath, simply saying, "Bastards," letting it out.

***

"If we're gonna get out of here, we need a diversion," George said to the group. "That was Quimby just run across the street with that Indian. He must be the marshal or whatever Quimby brought back with him. Any ideas on how to get those people thinking about something other than us?" he snarled, popping the cork on another bottle of whiskey.

"Fire works pretty good," one of the men said. Somebody else said, "Just start shootin'. They ain't that many of 'em." Many just stood staring at Sheridan George, waiting for him to say something.

"I like that idea of fire," he said. "Believe me, Pancho, there are a lot of them, so shooting our way out of this isn't realistic, at least right now." He was going to keep talking but was interrupted by activity on the street.

"Two men with a white flag coming onto the street in front of the Red Rose," somebody hollered from the front doors. "Looks like they want to talk. Maybe they like your idea of a trade with that little hotel feller."

Sheridan George jumped down from sitting on the bar, bottle still in his hand, and limped to the doors, his leg hurting from the horse's kick. "That's Quimby and the

Indian," he said, pushing his way through the doors. "That's far enough, Quimby. What do you want?"

"I'm Jose Red Feather, New Mexico Territorial Marshal," Red Feather said, "and Pete Quimby is my deputy for this section. You and your men have broken numerous territorial and federal laws. It is my responsibility to place you under arrest and hold you for trial.

"Please drop your weapons and come out onto the street." Both he and Quimby were smiling as Red Feather said that. Sheridan George was storming, and like the fool he was drew his weapon. Rifles and handguns opened up from the Red Rose and livery, but George dove through the doors of the Hearts of Gold, one bullet shattering his right elbow, forcing him to drop his weapon. Red Feather and Pete Quimby made it back inside the Red Rose unscathed.

George was howling with pain, trying to stop the bleeding, his arm hanging useless at his side. "Hold still and let me get a bandage wrapped on that," one of the men said, coming forward with a bar towel. "Got to stop the bleeding," he said, wrapping it tight and tying it off. "That was a lot of guns shootin' out there," he muttered, making sure the bandage would hold.

"Two of you men put together some torches and sneak over to that livery and burn it to the ground." George was livid with anger and pain, and he had consumed enough strong liquor to put two men in bed, all contributing to a lack of common sense on his part. "Two more of you, do the same thing to that hotel. We'll burn this damn town to the ground. They ain't gettin' me or what we have," he growled, holding his elbow. "Go now, damn it," he barked, and four men worked their way toward the back of the building. He stood up on weak knees and started toward the stairs leading to Holiday's office. He had to use the bannister for leverage and balance, weaving his way into the office.

Burn this damn place to the ground, he kept saying to himself, then the realization started making its way through the whiskey fog. *Got to get the gold out first. Got to get that gold out of this building, get it somewhere safe. Holiday, you son of a bitch, what have you got me into?* He plunked down at the desk, and this time, did not tip the bottle of whiskey, instead threw it across the room, breaking it, spilling fine bourbon on beautiful carpet. He laid his head down, passing out, drooling onto the desk.

***

"Just about what I expected," Red Feather said as Quimby and he dove through the front hanging doors of the Red Rose. "Now we're on level ground and know the rules," he chuckled, untying the white cloth from his rifle, accepting a cup of coffee from Reynaldo Cortez. "How would you get out of the mess if you were Holiday?" he asked, sitting back at the table.

"Fire," Rose Flannigan said, softly, terror in her eyes. "He'll try to burn us out." She looked at Quimby for a moment. "Pete, we haven't seen Holiday for hours, only that fool George. Do you think George would kill him?"

"No doubt," he said, shaking his head yes. "Sheridan George is a blood thirsty killer, wanted in several states and territories, and if Holiday is dead, George will do anything to protect all the gold and money that must be inside the saloon and down the street at the bank.

"As to fire," he continued, looking at each person at the table one at a time, "I think you are absolutely right. Wish we had some kind of communication with Pitts at the livery and Sloan at the bank."

"We do," Josh Pitts piped up from his place at the bar. "My dad always gets on me because I know how to get into places all over Plainsville. I can get messages to Dad and to Mr. Sloan."

"What Josh just said is true," Rose Flannigan said. "Bill has said that Josh has told him many times about what

163

goes on in Holiday's saloon, and I know that Don Jenkins and Josh used to play games with each other."

"Yeah," Josh said, looking down at the floor. "He knew all kinds of tricks about moving around town without being seen. He was a Texas Ranger, you know." He stopped for a minute, just staring at the floor, then said, "I can get to the livery and the bank without being seen. Yes I can."

Red Feather looked at Quimby, then Cortez. "We need to let Pitts and Sloan know what we're doing and what to watch for, but I'm not sure I want to send a young boy to do the job." He was shaking his head, then looked up at the young man. "Josh, you might run into some of Holiday's men. What would you do then? They are armed killers, outlaws with bounties on their heads. Wouldn't think twice about killing you. What would you do?"

Josh straightened himself up, stood tall and had a fierce look on his face. "I'm a man, Red Feather. I wouldn't go out there, wouldn't sneak around town with messages, unless I had my rifle with me. Mr. Jenkins taught me how to shoot and I'm very good, and there isn't anyone else here that could do the job." He looked around the saloon, noticed that many of the men were shaking their heads in agreement with what he said.

"Tell me what to tell Dad and Mr. Sloan, and I'll do it, and I'll bring messages back to you. Will I be scared, damn right I will be," and there was a distinct color to his face as he said that, "but I'm your man, Red Feather."

Rose looked like she wanted to say something, tell Josh no, you can't go, wanted Quimby to say no, wanted Red Feather to not let him go, but in her heart, she knew Josh Pitts would go, would do the job well. "Josh, be careful. Don't get hurt," she said, so softly, tears running down her cheeks, eyes wide open, looking at the boy. "You're the bravest boy-man I've ever known," and she swept him up in her arms, squeezing him until he had to try to break free.

"Gosh," he said, stepping back, red in the face. She put both hands on his shoulders, squeezed again, and went back to the table, crying softly. "I'll be careful," is all Josh said, just as quietly, following her to the table.

Red Feather told Josh what he wanted Pitts and Sloan to know, made sure the young man understood fully, and sent him off. "There goes one of your town's future leaders, Pete," Red Feather said, watching Josh, his rifle in hand, head out the back door of the saloon.

***

Young Pitts surveyed the area outside the saloon before stepping out and working his way around obstacles like buildings, trees, and possible killers. He was deep in some bushes, spread eagled when he spotted two men leaving the Hearts of Gold Saloon from a stand of trees several yards away, and watched as they gathered dry hay and weeds, and tied them to dry tree branches.

"They're making torches," he muttered, sinking deeper into the weeds under the trees. *I need to get this message to dad,* he thought, *but I can't let these men burn down the town.* He brought his rifle up, very slowly jacked a round into the receiver, and took long slow aim at the man holding the torch. As the second man drenched the torch in kerosene, Josh pulled the trigger, jacked another round in, aimed quickly, and killed the second man. The torch was never lit, and Josh was gone in seconds, hightailing it toward the livery.

He came in the back way, through the area where the lumber mill was being established, and through a line of corrals, entering the barn from the north. Tears were streaming down his cheeks, his nose was running, and he threw his arms around his father, crying as he had never cried before. "I killed two men, Dad," he blubbered. "They were going to burn the town down. I killed them," he moaned, as Bill Pitts hugged him tight, using his bandanna to wipe tears, letting the boy cry it out.

Pitts gave him his head, let him sob for a couple of minutes, and as the sobs eased off, Josh straightened himself up, wiped his nose again, and told everyone what Red Feather and Quimby had said. "Quimby was certain that there is no way to prepare food at that saloon, no way to store food, and their water comes from that well in the back, where those two men were making torches.

"Red Feather said the idea is to not let anyone leave that building, even if it takes two or three days. He said they will be hungry soon, and try to get out. I have to get down to the bank now and tell Mr. Sloan about this, also." The tears were gone, and Bill Pitts realized he was being talked to by a fourteen year old man, and the pride and fear swept through him.

Josh took a long drink of water, wiped his face with a wet rag, nodded to his father and all the men in the office, and slipped out the back of the barn. He circled way out and around the stockyards, coming back into town from the same south trail that Sloan used, creeping up to the bank door without being seen.

The door opened suddenly and Josh found himself looking down the wide, black open holes of a double barrel shotgun. "Don't shoot," he gulped. "It's me, Josh," terror written deep in his young face. "I have news from Pete Quimby." He was jerked into the bank by Charlie Sloan, who took the hammers off full cock on the scattergun after closing the big door of the bank.

"You just took a hell of a chance, Josh," Sloan said, glaring at the boy. "Those men out there are killers, boy."

Josh stood tall, looked Sloan in the eye and reminded him that if it wasn't for him none of these men would be here. "And, I ain't a boy, neither," he finished. He looked around the room, seeing the banker, Henry Swanson tied to a chair, his face black and blue, his nose bleeding, and his eyes almost puffed close.

"Red Feather and Quimby want everyone to set up so that the entire Hearts of Gold is covered with rifles and pistols, and not let anyone out of the building. Quimby is sure there's no food, and they have to go outside to get water. He said it might take a few days, but they will quit."

"I'd rather they made a run for it," Sloan said, a crooked smile splashed across his grizzled face. "Pick 'em off like turkeys or rabbits, one at a time. Shoot 'em in the gut, not kill 'em outright, make 'em suffer. That's what I say, but I know Pete's right. Take 'em prisoner, make them suffer for their crimes.

"Ok, boy, I mean, Josh, young Mr. Pitts," and he smiled at Josh, tousled his hair, "you get back to the Red Rose, and tell Pete we understand. Tell him, no, instead," and Sloan dashed into the banker's office and grabbed some papers. "You take these to Pete and make him read page two of the blank document. He'll understand.

"Now, scat, Josh, and stay safe," and they opened the door just wide enough for Josh to slip through and get back out of town on the south trail. He was back in the Red Rose in less than half an hour, winded but safe.

"Mr. Sloan said to read page two," Josh said, handing the mortgage paper to Pete Quimby.

Chapter Eighteen

"I don't like this just sitting around waiting for those fools to try something," Charlie Sloan said, walking, nay, pacing around the spacious new bank reception area. "Quimby's right, damn it, starving them out, but sure as hell they are going to try to do something horrible while they're starving." Every time he walked by Henry Sorenson he cuffed him across the head, sometimes on the back of the head, sometimes a direct slap to the face.

"So everybody that took out a loan unwillingly signed that second page without looking at it, then Holiday and George had them killed, and the bank, meaning you, Holiday, and George owned the property involved. You are one miserable son of a bitch," and Sorenson got slapped again.

Sorenson was bleeding from both ears and his nose, his lips were split and bleeding, his eyes were turning an ugly purple, and every joint and muscle in his body hurt. He left a job that was questionable at the Bank of California in Virginia City to work again with Thornton Holiday. *I'm the best front man he ever knew,* Sorenson was thinking. *I set up banks in Missouri, Texas, Reno, and was working to set up the bank in Virginia City when he told me about this grand plan. Your grand plan is going to get me killed,* he was crying to himself. *It sounded so good, and we own ranches, a saloon, a bank, stores in town, and other property is just a gunshot away. What went wrong?* he sobbed quietly.

"Let's get back at those fools," Sloan said, gathering everyone around him. "Quimby has their water source guarded and they have no food that we know of. They have a large store of whiskey, maybe a keg or two of beer, and that's it. Without becoming targets, how can we intimidate them, make their lives hell in that palace Holiday built?"

It was very quiet for several long minutes, the men looking at each other, shaking their heads. "Yeah, me too," Sloan said. "Without just marching down the street and getting picked off like ducks on the lake, I think the best bet is just sit it out, as much as that thought galls me."

***

Bill Pitts was hunkered down with Sonny Bergstrom and Kirk Taylor, trying to see if they could create some kind of action against the Holiday gang at the saloon. "No matter what we come up with," Pitts said, "it puts one or more of us in jeopardy, and there is no reason for that."

Bergstrom shook his head slowly, finally stood up from the table and walked to the window, staring at the saloon across the way. "If I had my way, I'd say, let's storm the place, but I know Pete's right. Starve 'em out, nobody gets hurt or dead. I keep wondering what Dave Peterson would have done, or John Morton.

"Well, I think our best bet is to just continue to keep them penned up. It should drive 'em nuts after awhile." He raised his rifle and put a round into the Hearts of Gold Saloon, spit some tobacco juice out the window, and smiled slightly. "Did that just because I could," he said, turning back to the group. They smiled, knowing his frustration.

***

"You have Worry and another man guarding the back door of Holiday's saloon?" Quimby asked and Reynaldo Cortez nodded yes. "And we have a few men upstairs in the hotel looking out front and back windows?" again getting the affirmative nod. "I guess our bases are pretty well covered, then," he muttered.

"I'm so damn mad right now, I'd like to set a case of dynamite off under Holiday's butt," he said, pacing around the roomy saloon. "Rose, I signed that second page too, just like Peterson and Morton and Jenkins. It was a death warrant, and I just went right along with the sheep.

"What kind of man is it that would even come up with a plan like this? How on earth could anyone expect to carry it off? Eventually, when there are no more property owners in the town, somebody would get wise." He laughed at himself when he realized what he said. "Well, you know what I meant," he said, continuing his pacing.

"Have you ever run into anything like this, Red Feather?"

"Nope, never. I've been chasing outlaws for a long time and I've never heard of anything like this. Unbelievable. Holiday had to think he was setting up some kind of outlaw kingdom, had to believe that bank robbers and murderers would want to run a ranch or some kind of business, and live in peace. The man was simply insane and Sheridan George was too stupid to have recognized it, and Henry Sorenson only saw himself as a banker, wealthy beyond belief.

"Holiday put together a whole gaggle of stupid, selfish, murderous people, and Pete, he almost got away with it. Another few months and there wouldn't have been anyone around Plainsville to complain. Without you and Rose Flannigan raising as much dust as you did, he would have gotten away with it."

It got very quiet in the Red Rose Saloon after that little speech, Pete Quimby looking at Rose Flannigan, then back at Red Feather. "That's frightening," is all Quimby could say, sitting down at a table. "He was banking on nobody taking the extra few seconds to look at that second page. We are as much to blame as he," he snarled, standing and pacing around the room. He looked at each person as he said, "Didn't your daddy tell you never sign anything you didn't read? Yeah, mine too," he said with a stupid grin on his face.

"Is there some way we could hurry this 'wait them out' process?" Reynaldo Cortez asked, pouring yet another cup of boiling coffee. "If it's already getting old and cramped for us, it must be working on them over there, too," he said, itching for a fight. "Is there something we can do to get this started? What would drive a hungry man to do something stupid?"

Josh Pitts cocked his head at that thought and stood up. "What's the one thing that will always make your mouth water? You're all cattlemen. Come on, think about it. Take a side of beef and put it on a spit over a bed of coals. I bet your mouth is already watering. Mine is," he grinned, pretending to chew on a long rib bone.

"That boy's gonna be governor, Pete. You listen to that? It's brilliant." Red Feather and Reynaldo Cortez bumped shoulders, Pete whopped Josh on the back, and Old Pete pretended to be cutting a slab of roasted beef from the grilling side of beef.

"Do you have a beef at the livery, Josh?" Red Feather asked, bringing immediate quiet to the room.

"I've been raising one for the Fourth of July celebration," he said, smiling. "We'll just pretend it's the Fourth," he continued. "Dad and I built that large brick stove with the spit just for celebrations. We've cooked a side of beef every year, and I can't think of anything that smells better than roasting beef on open coals. Nothing," he said, jumping up from a chair.

"Let me get over to the livery and we'll get started. This place is gonna smell so good in a couple of hours those outlaws will crawl out with their hands up to get a slab of good beef."

He hoisted his rifle, checked to make sure there was a round in the receiver, and headed out the door for the livery. "I'll be careful," he said with a grin, before anyone had a chance to tell him to. He stopped at the well to check on Worry and the Peterson hand with him, and told them the plan.

"There's an idea that will drive old Holiday mad,

for sure. Have a town-wide celebration including a roasted side of beef on a spit," and old Worry cackled and slapped his knee. "Why not have some music, too," he howled in fun, pretending that he wanted to dance with Josh. "That's the best plan I've ever heard," he said.

"Is that really you talkin'," the grizzled old ranch hand said. "Nothing to worry about, Worry?" he asked, half in jest, winking at Josh Pitts. "Right now, I don't care if the plan works or not, I'm just gonna sit here and protect this well, and wait for a slab or spit roasted beef to be delivered," and he finally let his own laughter out.

"Well, I better get over to the livery and get this party underway," Josh quipped, slinking away from the water well, back into the trees and the long way around to the stables. As he neared the edge of a stand of quaking Aspen, he spotted two men moving toward the stables. He didn't recognize either one. He followed, staying well behind and out of sight as they worked their way around the new mill site, and toward the corrals.

Each man carried a rifle and wore side arms, keeping a low profile as they moved. *We're too far away for me to yell a warning,* Josh thought, feeling a chill spread through his body. He could vision the two men he killed earlier, knew he might just have to do it again. *I'm going to have to shoot those men,* and he could almost feel the tears begin to well up.

No! he said to himself. *I have to. If I don't, someone in the livery is going to get shot or die. I'm a man, and this is what men have to do,* and he dropped down on one knee, brought the rifle up, pulled the hammer back and took a long aim at the man in front. The second shot was harder as the second man tried to duck into the cover of the surrounding brush. He didn't make it.

"What was that?" Kirk Taylor said, whirling around from his position near the open window in the livery office.

"Sounded like rifle fire, out the back," Bill Pitts

172

said, hightailing it out the door, that big shotgun in hand. Bergstrom followed, motioning Taylor to stay put at the window. Pitts and Bergstrom ran through the large barn just in time to see Josh running as fast as he could through the corrals.

"Two men were sneaking through the brush toward the corrals," he sputtered after his long run, tears streaming across his face. "I had to do it again, Dad," he cried, but stood straight and tall as he told what had happened. "When this is over," he said, quietly, "I won't ever shoot anything again. Ever." Bill Pitts put his arm around his son and they walked back into the office.

"You're the bravest young man I've ever known," Pitts said, giving Josh a glass of water. "Did you bring some more information?"

Josh perked right up after taking half a glass of water down. "I sure did," he exclaimed. "We're gonna have a party." He walked over to the table and sat down, inviting Bill and Sonny to join him. "Now, what is it that would make Holiday lay down his gun and walk right out of that old saloon over there," he smiled. "They're getting hungry over there, and several hours from now, they'll really be hungry.

"So," he continued, Pitts and Bergstrom leaning forward to hear what the lad was talking about. "So," he said again, "we're gonna slaughter that steer we're saving for the Fourth of July celebration, and roast a side on the spit. If roasting beef on an open bed of coals won't bring those jaspers out of that saloon, nothing will," he laughed, bouncing up and down on the chair.

"Well, I'll be damned," Sonny Bergstrom said, looking over at Kirk Taylor, "this kid is something. What a great idea." He looked at Bill Pitts, then at Josh, got up and walked to the door. "You just gonna sit there, or give me a hand with that steer?"

An hour later, great logs of oak and other

hardwood were burning down to coals, a side of beef was strapped to the spit and lifted into place.

"We'll take turns with the spit," Bill Pitts said, "and I'm first." He slipped the handle into place and tightened it to the axel of the spit, slowly starting to turn several hundred pounds of corral raised beef. "Those boys are gonna be so hungry they'll beg to give themselves up," he laughed. "Maybe somebody ought to find a fiddle or mandolin and we can have some music while this beef is cooking," and Josh laughed the loudest.

"That's exactly what Worry said," and he tried to get Sonny Bergstrom to dance.

***

"Gunshots," Gomez, one of Sloan's men said. "Sounds like it's out behind the livery. Maybe some of Holiday's people are movin' around." From the open door of the bank, he could see the Plainsville Hotel and Red Rose Saloon, the Emporium just across the street, and at the far end of the street, the livery and stables. The Hearts of Gold Saloon was around the corner from the livery and out of sight.

"I'd sure feel more comfortable if we were all down at the Red Rose," Charlie said, glancing out the doorway. "But, sure as hell, if we took old Swanson and went down there, Holiday would pick that time to make his move and hit the bank on his way out of town."

He chuckled some, thinking about what he just said. "Not many bank robbers I've heard of, robbed their own bank," and some of the others chuckled as well. "No, we better just stay right here, keep this yahoo alive so he can hang, and protect the money that's in the bank."

Gomez pointed out the door. "Looks like smoke coming from the corrals, behind the barn. Something's on fire back there." Several of the men in the bank gathered and watched blue smoke drift across the livery, toward the Hearts of Gold Saloon and the Red Rose. "What the heck

174

are they doin'?" Gomez said, then spotted Josh Pitts coming around from the back of the bank.

"What's goin' on?" Sloan demanded, as Josh came in. "Heard gunshots, see smoke, what's goin' on?" Sloan was the kind of man that thrived on action, knowing what needed to be done and doing it. For several hours, he's been cooped up in the bank, knowing a bunch of outlaws were less than two hundred yards away, and he knew he was one of those responsible for them being there.

"Damn it," he snarled, stomping around the floor, "We have the people and the guns, let's get those yahoos."

"The smoke you see is going to get them out of that saloon real soon," Josh said, taking a seat in one of the plush chairs to be used by bank customers waiting their turn to be fleeced by Swanson and Holiday. "The fire is in the roasting pit Dad and I built, and we slaughtered our Fourth of July steer. When that side of beef starts cooking real good, and those outlaws in the saloon know how hungry they are and smell that roast beef, they'll beg us to let them give up." He was having a hard time not guffawing, and many of the men in the bank were smiling, just watching him.

"Well, now," Charlie Sloan said, "that's a plan I like. Can't remember the last time I had something to eat, now that I think about it." He did some more pacing around the large bank reception area, head bent in thought. "Any of several things could come from this. They could just give up, but Holiday and George don't strike me as the givin' up kind. On the other hand, those with them might rebel, and that would be fun to watch," he smiled, saying it.

"No, Josh, I don't think those outlaws are going to just give up, but I think it's the best plan we have. It will create problems inside that saloon of theirs, and for us, it's gonna be a lot better to have them fighting amongst themselves than fighting us. Yes sir, it's a good plan."

Chapter Nineteen

T he only thing on George's mind was getting that gold out of the saloon building and into a hiding place he could return to when this mess is cleared up. He didn't see the impending end as anything more than being able to get out alive. "Let's get two men over to that barn and set it on fire," he stormed, pointing at the Pitts' Livery and Blacksmith Works. "That fire will keep these fools busy long enough for us to get out. A bounty of one hundred dollars for whoever lights it up," he snarled.

Two men stepped forward immediately. "Good, one hundred each when I see that place on fire and you're back here. Get going," he said, and they headed toward the back door of the Hearts of Gold Saloon. Garrison, his rifle in hand led the way down the hallway, Warren just a step or two behind.

"They's been a lot of gunfire from back here," Garrison said. "Wish there was another way out." Two bodies were still half in and half out of the building, simply left to rot by George. "Them two didn't even make it out the door."

"There's a cellar," Warren said, tapping his partner on the shoulder. "Follow me," and he turned into a short hallway that ended in a staircase leading down to a storeroom filled with kegs of alcoholic beverages. "This is where the whiskey is watered down and the wine and stuff is kept." He walked across the room, and took a ramp up to large wooden doors that would allow a wagon to be unloaded into the cellar. There was a man-way door in one of the large doors.

"Careful now," Warren said, getting the man door open slightly. He couldn't see anyone and motioned for Garrison to follow him as he slipped out and stayed low, running for some trees lining the street. The two worked their way through several stands of trees and bushes, toward the back of the corrals. "That's where Pitts is building his lumber mill," Warren pointed out. "If we skirt around that, we can get close to the barn and burn it out."

"What I'd rather do is just steal a damn horse from one of the corrals and get the hell out of this mess. I don't see anything but being killed if I stay. Hundred dollars ain't worth it," Garrison said, staring at corrals, most filled with fine horses. "None of us is gonna get out alive, Warren. You know that."

"Ain't never run out on a man, before," Warren said. "Sheridan George is a mean one, Garrison."

"I don't think I'da thought about runnin' out on old Holiday, but I ain't got no love for George. He's a murderin' fool, and I'm not willing to die for him." They were standing close enough that they could sneak through the bushes, into one of the closer corrals, lead a couple of horses out quietly, and be gone in two minutes. A rifle shot dropped Garrison first, and as Warren tried to dive into some bushes, a second shot killed him.

"Sounds like I saved two hundred dollars," George snarled, pacing about the saloon, glaring at anyone he caught looking at him. He went down the hallway leading to the back door and found the entrance to the cellar storeroom door open. *What's this? I didn't know this even existed,* he said to himself, walking down the stairway into the large storeroom. *I'll be damned. Look at the size of this room and all this liquor. I can get my gold out using that ramp. We kill Quimby and that redhead, and I can get a wagon, and save all my gold.* He spent about half an hour looking at every square foot of the warehouse.

As he walked out of the passage, back into the hallway leading to the saloon, he could hear the men talking about smoke at the livery. *Maybe those fools made it after all,* he mused. "What's all the fuss," he said, as he neared the front door without making himself a target for the shooter at the stables.

"Looks like a fire behind the livery barn, George," one man piped up, pointing at smoke curling up.

"Not much of a fire," George said, "considering all the hay and wood around there. They'll have that out in no time. They ain't gettin' their hundred bucks, if they make it back. It must have been them shootin'." He walked back to the bar and poured another glass of whiskey.

"We need to clear them people out of that hotel and livery, get Swanson out of the bank and safe, and burn this damn town to the ground. Holiday was wrong. His plan still doesn't make any sense," George growled, sucking down another half glass of whiskey. "Should never have listened to him."

Some of the men had separated themselves from the main group, watching George drink considerable amounts of whiskey. "Even though that stuff is half water, he's had enough to drop most men," Whitey said, as George took another drink of the amber heat. "I'm ready to make my play," he said, looking to see if the others were still with him.

They had been planning to challenge George for several hours, and were waiting to see if he would simply get drunk, making the job that much easier. "He doesn't seem to ever get drunk," one of the men said.

"He's drunk," Whitey said. "He ain't talking straight and sure as hell ain't thinking straight. I can take him, but we'll have to fight off some of these other yahoos, also. You sure you're ready?" he asked, looking at each of the others. They all nodded yes, and Whitey took a step or two toward Sheridan George.

***

"Looks like Josh made it to the stables," Red Feather said, watching smoke drifting over the top of the livery. "That boy's got more spunk than I've seen in a long time. Better stay on his good side, Pete," he chuckled. "That boy's going places."

Several people had gathered at the entrance to the saloon, watching the progress of the roasting fire at the livery. "Once they get that side of beef tied off and on the spit, the aroma should drift right into Holiday's little complex over there." Quimby had a smile on his face watching the blue smoke curl and drift toward the Hearts of Gold Saloon.

"I'm hoping this ends tonight, Red Feather. Rose Flannigan and several of us have put together the makings of a town, and it would be nice to get that started just as soon as this nest of outlaws is cleared out and gone." He seemed contemplative for a moment or two before continuing.

"The governor was right. Plainsville is just a place, not a real town. Without us creating the real thing, that railroad will never come through; the town will never build into the community so many of us want. There are good people here, Red Feather, people who have built their lives, their families, their businesses.

"Right now," Quimby continued, his eyes sparkling, his jaw set, "we are in a position that few people ever will know. We can build a town the way we want the town to be. Imagine that, Red Feather. It's ours to build."

"One of the first things you will have to do, Pete, is declare that Plainsville exists. Then create a town council, simply by declaration, and that council will have to appoint a justice of the peace and a sheriff. That can all be done in a quickly called public meeting, maybe even as we finish off a side of beef tomorrow at dinner," and everyone laughed along with the big Indian lawman.

"After that, put the survivors of this gang in jail, then take whatever time is necessary to finalize the creation of the town, get the paperwork off to Santa Fé, and you're in business."

"Sounds too easy, Red Feather," said Rose Flannigan, standing at the table with Reynaldo Cortez.

"The process sounds easy, but it will take an immense amount of time after the initial declaration. It has to be legal and binding, and then it will still have to be accepted by the territorial legislature and governor. But, remember this, you are doing the right thing, and doing it the right way. Everyone involved should be damn proud of that."

Old Pete took it on himself to ring the bell, catching Rose by surprise, but she smiled and gave her ok. Everyone slid up to the bar and Pete poured whatever they wanted, in honor of their new town.

"Well, look who's here," Rose said, a big smile spread across her Irish face. "Charlie Sloan. What brings you to town?" she joked, giving the big cowboy a generous hug. "Please don't tell us there's a problem down at the bank."

"The only problem is, that fool banker is still alive," he said, and there was no smile or chuckle along with the statement. "No, no problem," he said, calming down a bit. "Josh told us what is going to happen, but I'm worried about the rest of the town. Pete, you put people in really good strategic places, but the rest of the town isn't aware of what we're doing." He took the mug of cold beer offered by Old Pete, and quaffed it in two gulps.

"I've wanted a cold beer ever since we rode into town," and this time there was a smile on his rough old face. "Anyway, this town was ready to back you for sheriff, Pete, and I'm sure if they knew what was going on, they would better be able to protect themselves."

"He's right," Red Feather said, immediately. "Keeping Holiday and his gang tied up in that saloon is taking most of the people we have," he said. "How do we get word of what we're doing to those in their homes? Some little lady who decides to take a walk to the mercantile shop or the café could be in serious danger.

"How many men do you have at the bank?"

"There's me and four others. Me and one other feller could handle the bank. That would allow three men to fan out and spread the word among the rest of the folk." Charlie motioned for another beer, which Old Pete poured right away. "That makes me feel better," he said, then laughing, said, "Yeah, the beer and making the rest of the town's people safe."

Charlie Sloan started to leave, to head back to the bank, when a series of gunshots rang out at the Hearts of Gold Saloon. "That's a lot of gunfire," Red Feather stated. "Might mean they're fighting among themselves, which will save us the trouble, if that's the case. Keep an eye on the place, Pete. I'm going to see how close I can get, maybe find out what's going on over there."

He slipped out the front of the saloon, edged along the side of the building and disappeared around the corner. Quimby and Sloan stood near the doorway, rifles in hand, ready to shoot the first person to move. "I better head back," Sloan said, slipping out the door, going the other way.

"If Holiday has eyes on us," Quimby said, "he'll think something's up, watching two men head out in two different directions. Reynaldo, do a quick check on all your people, around the back, upstairs in the hotel, wherever you have them." Cortez moved out to check on his people.

"Sit with me a minute, Rose," Pete said, holding a chair for her at one of the tables. "Looks like you and Rey Cortez are getting rather close," he said, a smile crossing his face.

"He's a wonderful man, Pete. We've had feelings for some time but neither one of us did anything about them. All at once we were forced into being close and those feelings just exploded. I'm glad you noticed. Are you all right with it?"

He took her hand and gave it a squeeze. "Only if Rey will let me be the best man."

***

"Wow, somebody's shooting up a storm over there," Sonny Bergstrom said, standing near the livery office window. "That sounded like five or six shots, all at once. Maybe they be fightin' with each other," he said, keeping his rifle at the ready. Several others, Pitts and Taylor included came over to see if they could see anything.

"That big roast of beef out there ought to be smelling pretty good, soon," Bill Pitts said, walking back out to tend the spit. "Make sure nobody sneaks up on me while I'm wrestling with that spit. The beef is heavy."

"I'll come out with you, Bill," Kirk Taylor said. "Give old Sonny a chance to shoot somebody through that window. I got my man," he snickered, getting a mean look back from Bergstrom.

"You think they might be fightin' among themselves?" Bergstrom asked, keeping that rifle at the ready. "Might make it easier if there be fewer of 'em. Taylor was kinda joshin' there, but he's right. I do want to shoot more than one of them fools. They killed about the best boss I ever rode for. Dave Peterson was a cattleman and horseman from way back, and they killed him.

"Yeah, I do want to shoot some of those bastards. All of 'em," he snarled, and sent a round into the saloon, just because he could. Pitts and Taylor were laughing as they walked out to tend the spit.

Chapter Twenty

"If that barn is on fire, it ain't much of a fire," George said again, walking around the saloon. Sheridan George was thinking more about how to get the gold out of the building and hidden so he could come back for it. His mind addled by a large quantity of liquor, he was mis-reading the men around him. "Can't anybody do a decent job around here? How hard is it to burn down a barn?"

"You got yourself a bad attitude, George," Whitey said, slouching against one of the support columns near the faro table. "What makes you think you're runnin' things, anyway? We signed on with Holiday, and just cuz you killed him don't make you the boss." Whitey was tall and skinny, known by the men as a bank robber and cattle thief, he wore his sidearm low, and with long arms, could whip it out fast.

"I think we need to worry more on how to get out of this fouled up plan of Holiday's than getting' even with a redheaded woman that throwed you out of her saloon," and he laughed, right in George's face. That's all it took, and George made his move.

As Whitey taunted George, those standing around him spread out some, watching the other outlaws. Some moved away from the impending fight, others gravitated toward Sheridan George, and some toward Whitey and his friends. George was known as one of the fastest men to clear leather, and his hand was a blur as the big revolver came up, fire and lead belching from the big bore.

Whitey was fast as well, and his Colt erupted at the same time. George took a round in his shoulder, Whitey took one in the leg, both men on the floor in pain, but that was not the end of the fight. George's backers slapped leather, Whitey's friends slapped leather, and the saloon filled with blue smoke and death. Whitey, gun in hand fired twice more at George's people, but George was done for. His elbow shattered, now suffering a wound to his shoulder, the combination of blood loss, pain, and alcohol was more than his system could take, and he lay unconscious on the barroom floor.

Two of Whitey's friends died, three of George's did too, and the two sides stood staring at each other, guns drawn, deciding whether or not to continue the fight. Leon Kennedy, one of Whitey's backers finally said, "All right, let's stop it right now," and slowly slipped his Colt in its leather. All the others, both sides, did the same thing, warily, slowly, and calm returned to the Hearts of Gold.

"Let's tend to those that need it and think about how the hell we're gonna get out of this mess. They got a lot more guns out there than we do, and they got us surrounded besides. George and Holiday ain't in this, now, and all their brave talk about an outlaw haven ain't gonna happen, so how do we get out of this alive?"

Several of the men moved to the bar and poured drinks, talking among themselves, little arguments ending quickly. No one paid any attention to the wounded and dead. Kennedy spoke up again. "Holiday had a lot of money, here at the saloon, and down at that bank. Now," he rolled out in his Texas drawl, "I think the bank's out, but I'll bet there's money here that we could split and then see if we can slip out of this mess.

"Let's just take a few minutes to find that money, split it up, and then figure out what to do." He had sidled up to the bar as he was talking and poured a drink. "Whitey, you gonna be ok to ride if we can steal some horses?"

Whitey had moved to one of the cocktail tables and was sitting in a chair, wrapping a ripped shirt around his leg wound. "Yeah, I'm fine, Leon. Go find that money." Any thoughts of Sheridan George were set aside in favor of a search for money, gold, and maybe a way out.

***

When the gunfire erupted, Quimby moved to the door of the Red Rose, looking to see if Red Feather was involved. "See anything?" Reynaldo asked, coming with him.

"Can't see Red Feather, and there ain't anyone running out of Holiday's place. Maybe they're shooting each other," Quimby said. "That would be good." He was standing just inside the door, saw the smoke curling up from the roasting pit, but couldn't see any movement anywhere in the town. "Hope Red Feather wasn't the target of all that shooting," he said, moving back into the saloon.

"It'll take another half hour or so before that beef starts really smelling good," Reynaldo said, "and I'll wager those fools over there are pretty hungry right now. They won't realize how hungry they are until they smell that roasting meat. Just talking about it and I'm hungry."

"Because of Rosie at the café, we've been eating, have plenty of hot coffee, and of course a cold beer once in a while," Quimby said, "so, we're not going to be affected as much by that roast beef, but those boys over there, it will be rough on them. I think it's time to start making a plan on how to roust them out of there when it starts smelling really good."

He put several of the tables together and chairs all around and invited everyone to sit down. He indicated that one of the men stay near the front to keep an eye on Holiday's place. "Those men are mean, they are outlaws, probably each one has killed a man before, so this won't be easy," Quimby said as everyone settled in. "It sounds good, but we can't just assume that because they're hungry and that roast beef smells so good, that they will roll over and quit. I don't think that for a second. Ain't gonna happen. But if we play it long and slow, force them to endure those good smells, I think eventually they will want to quit."

Cortez, sitting next to Rose, said, "I think they're

gonna make a run for it, Pete. I think that's what all that gunfire was about, some wanting to fight it out, some wanting to run for it. Holiday and George, both known killers, will want to fight it out, Holiday to protect what he's built here, George because he's Holiday's wolf, his killer pet. And, we don't know how many there are."

"That's what Red Feather was trying to find out," Pete said. "I sure hope he wasn't involved in that gunfight."

"I wasn't," Red Feather said, coming in the back way of the saloon, a big smile splashed across his face, "but thanks for the thought." He walked up to the table, spun a chair around backward, and sat down. "I was close enough to know what's going on, though," he said, accepting a cup of hot coffee from Old Pete.

"This your coffee, or Rosie's?" he asked, remembering Old Pete's coffee had long legs and strong muscles. Old Pete just sniffed, trying to say his feeling's were hurt, and walked away. Red Feather chuckled, and continued. "I was close enough to the side of that building to hear them talking. It looks like Sheridan George killed Holiday some time ago, and is now out of the game, probably bleeding to death.

"The rest of the gang, and their numbers are down to around ten or so, are tearing the building apart looking for Holiday's money. They plan to split it up and then try to break out. During the split, I would imagine there will be some good fights, and the numbers will be even less. The only person left who really knows what the overall plan was is the banker, so if we plan to try to figure out who owns what, when this is over, we must keep him and his records safe."

"We were talking about that," Quimby said, "about creating the town, creating legal officials, and what to do with whatever is left. That money in the bank could become seed money for the Plainsville Township, but the properties that the bank says it owns, will have to be distributed very carefully."

"I don't know anything about Morton's ranch or Jenkins' store, but Dave Peterson always said he wanted his ranch to go to his hands. The problem with that is, even though all of us heard him say it, many times, I'll bet it was never written down. The telegraph company owns the building Tater lived and worked in, and they'll need to replace him. I think we're looking at many weeks of hard work once this is over."

"We all know pretty much what the town will be facing," Red Feather said, hugging the back of his chair, "so I think we need to concentrate on ending the problem quickly. How many people do you have guarding the well and back of Holiday's saloon?" he asked Cortez.

"Worry and Slim are out back, there's one man at the hotel back door, and two men upstairs in windows, one in front, one behind, in the hotel," he answered. "Right now, two Peterson hands are at the Livery along with Pitts and Josh, and I think Charlie Sloan has either three or four men with him. What are you thinking?"

Red Feather took a long swig of coffee, almost staring at the ceiling before answering. "If they try to break out, they will need horses, and if Holiday has as much money as I'm thinking, they will be carrying a load. Everything I'm thinking right now tells me there will be some huge fighting inside that saloon before they make their play. No matter what, they will have to concentrate on getting to the stables. Just about every horse in town, except for what we rode in on is in those corrals right now.

"Let's put two more men with Worry and Slim, get Charlie to bring Swanson down here to the Red Rose with his men, and send about half of them to the livery. What do you think, Pete? That cover the town?"

"I think so. My big worry will be fire. That saloon is wood from top to bottom as is most of the town, and remember, Josh Pitts stopped two men from burning the town down once already. If one gets started, it probably can't be stopped." He looked around the room, seeing that heads were shaking in agreement.

"As far as I know, only the two entrances, front and back exist, so what you're saying should cover any attempt to leave," Quimby said.

"No," Rose said, quickly. "Holiday put in a cellar. Josh told me about that, and there are large barn-like doors that lead into it so a wagon can be backed right up to the doors. It's on the far side of the building, with a couple of cottonwood trees almost hiding the entrance."

"That changes things," Red Feather said. "We'll need at least two people guarding that area. Maybe those two upstairs in the hotel? Will that work Rey?" Cortez nodded yes, Quimby nodded as well. "Good. Then let's get started, moving people and setting up for their break out. Cortez, get somebody down to the bank, and beef up the outside security around the well."

"You look rather satisfied," Quimby said to Red Feather. "Do you think this is almost over?"

"I think it's very close to being over, Pete. Holiday and George are out of the picture, and those that are left are just workers. They don't care what happens as long as they come out alive, and that's our ace. If they find some money, that will start fights and more will die, bringing the odds overwhelmingly in our favor.

"When hunger kicks in, fortified by a roasting beef on a spit, and we offer them a chance to live, it will be over. The really good thing, Pete," he said, as serious as Quimby has seen him, "you people are ready for that. You have a plan, written out, ready to be accepted by the governor and the territorial legislature."

"As much as I want that, I'm still fearful that the railroad won't think we're ready. That bothers me."

"I think a little chat with Governor Monahan will keep Ralph Flowers very much in the game. Plainsville will be a town with duly elected leaders, and the railroad will want to be a part of that."

"You're a positive influence, Red Feather," Pete Quimby said, giving the big Indian a light punch to the shoulder, both men smiling broadly.

"Smell that?" the man at the front door said. "Whoo-ee, I'm thinking this will be good. I want a steak this big," and his arms were wide open, "and this heavy," and pretended he couldn't hold it up.

Laughter rang out as the group moved from the tables to the front of the Red Rose Saloon, and took in the aroma of roasting beef as it wafted through the town. "I think Josh's plan is a good one," Rose said, standing close to Reynaldo Cortez.

"This problem will end soon, I think," Cortez said. "Hope someone brought a mandolin or fiddle. Roast beef, straight off the spit, a glass of cold beer, and some music to dance to will be a fitting end to Holiday's gang."

Chapter Twenty-One

L eon grabbed one of the men and headed upstairs to what had been Thornton Holiday's office, found the liquor bottles that George had emptied, and a couple that were still half full. Leon took a whiff. "This isn't what's at the bar," he said, tipping the bottle up. "This is sippin' whiskey straight from Kentucky, my friend. What my pappy used to 'still." He handed the other bottle to his companion and took a long look around the large, ornately decorated room.

"Holiday lived well," he muttered, spotting the safe with the thick steel door ajar. He pulled one of the heavy canvas bags out and untied the cord, turning the bag on its side, spilling several thousand or so dollars on the thick carpet. "Damn," was all he said, emptying the rest of the bag.

Henry Torrez slowly put the bottle down, whiskey dribbling off his stubble-covered chin. "George wasn't gonna tell us about this," he said slowly, picking a gold coin or two up, sinking his teeth into one of them. "It's gold."

Leon grabbed the other two sacks, emptied them, and the two just stood there, eyes gleaming, thinking of how many ways that much gold could be spent, how much trouble it would be to keep all the others from any of it, whether Leon could take Torrez, or the other way around. The big question was the same as George's; how the hell do we get it out of here?

"We need a good wagon and a team, Torrez," Leon said, knowing that wasn't going to happen. The two just stood surrounded by a large pile of twenty dollar gold pieces that for all the good they would get out of them might as well be horse puckey.

Footsteps and voices brought them around, and two men found them just standing in that pile of gold. "Holy shit," one of them said, the other walked back to the head of the stairs and called those down below to come up and see what Leon and Torrez had found. Of the original gang, only about ten or twelve were still alive, and within minutes, Holiday's office was filled with outlaws that had never seen that much loot. Ever.

Whitey had a hard time climbing the stairs and was the last one in. "So," he said, "Looks like Holiday did have a hoard. That's why George kept coming up here, trying to figure out how he could keep it all." He limped over to Holiday's large chair and plopped down.

"Anybody count that yet?" he drawled, giving the evil eye to a couple that seemed to be putting some in their pockets. "Nobody takes any until it's counted and divvied up."

"Who made you the boss?" one of those with gold coins in his pockets said, letting his hand drift toward the handle of his revolver. He didn't make it as Whitey pulled, cocked, and fired in a flash, and the outlaw and his gold was flung back against the hardwood-paneled wall, dead before he hit the carpet.

"We each get a share," Whitey said, that big hog leg still smoking and still in his hand. "At some point we will need to know how much there is, but I think making a plan to get out of here should come first. We will need good horses and there's only one place to get them. We'll need saddles and bridles, and large saddle bags to carry this stuff," he laughed, slowly lowering the hot iron into its holster.

Tension lifted slightly, but that mound of gold gleamed in every man's eye, and with another down and dead, each man's take got larger. "We'll have to take out those jaspers at the livery," Whitey said, "and bring the horses into that cellar. It will take several men, I think."

"Yeah, sure," one of the men piped up. "While we attack the livery, you sneak out with the gold. You want horses, you go get 'em," he said, and many heads were nodding in agreement. Some of the others were looking around, sizing up the men in the room, wondering if they could take them out. Whitey's original group was down to four men, and the other group, the ones with George, had maybe seven.

"What's that smell?" one of George's men said, sniffing at the air. "Smells like roasting meat," he said, almost as a question. Everybody started sniffing the air and slowly filed out of the office, down the stairs, and toward the front of the saloon. "It's coming from the livery," somebody said, pointing at the curling smoke that had been seen earlier.

"That smells good," one said, sticking his nose in the air, as a slow smile spread across his face. "Didn't realize how hungry I am. What the heck are they doing?" One of the men, in his effort to get a full whiff of the enticing aroma got too close to the bat-wing doors and took a rifle shot through the middle of his chest.

No one in the Hearts of Gold Saloon heard Sonny Bergstrom say something about, "no roast beef for you," as he jacked another round in his Henry. "Those boys are crowding the door over there," Bergstrom hollered out the open door toward where the spit was. "If it smells this good to us, it must be driving them crazy. I hope," he smirked.

Two men from Charlie Sloan's group arrived and told Pitts what Red Feather and Quimby were planning. "You can bet they will make a break for it of some kind, and the only way they can get out of town is to get their hands on some of these horses here. They sure as hell ain't walking out."

"Josh, take these gents around to the corrals, Kirk, why don't you go with him, and you four spread yourselves out to keep anyone from getting near the horses," Bill Pitts said.

"I'll bet that's what those other two were doin',"

Josh said, looking down at the ground, remembering the shooting. "They were after horses, not killing you." He grabbed his rifle and motioned the others to follow him. It only took a couple of minutes to set up a good defense between the horses and Holiday's saloon. Josh pointed out the two big doors, slightly hidden in the cottonwood grove.

"They open into a large cellar under the saloon. Big enough to drive a team and wagon in with supplies. Most people in town don't know about that, but I watched them dig out the cellar and build the saloon on top."

"That's where they'll come from when they make a break for the horses," Kirk Taylor said. "Is there anything going on in this town that you don't know about?" he joked with Joshua, thumping the young man on the shoulder. "Let's use the brush and trees for cover, and keep a close watch on that building."

"Any idea how many men might be left over there?" Josh asked, squirming down almost inside a large sage brush.

Taylor just shook his head. "Me and Sonny have knocked off quite a few, there's been lots of gunfire inside, and you took out four of 'em," he answered. "Can't be that many left. They'll either be ready to quit, soon, or they'll be desperate to escape. The smell from that roasting side of beef might help them decide," he smiled, tucking in behind a large cottonwood tree. "I hope your dad or Sonny, or somebody, brings us a couple of big steaks off that hunk of steer. It's making me hungry, for sure," he laughed.

In the saloon, Whitey had the body from upstairs and the one shot at the entrance, taken down the long hallway toward the back door. "If we wait 'till dark," he was saying to Leon, "we can make a break through those cellar doors, find some horses, and get the hell out of here."

"What about the gold?" Leon asked. "That's thousands of dollars, Whitey. We can't just leave it." His eyes told Whitey that Leon would not leave it. "I won't leave it."

The two were at a table away from most of the others. "Maybe we can use those big sacks and take some of it," Whitey said, "but sure as hell, we can't take all or even most of it. Just too heavy, Leon."

Whitey was a planner at heart, he'd arranged for more than twenty bank robberies in his career, could work out a way into a bank, and a way out of a town with the loot, but try as he might, getting even a small bag of that gold out of that office upstairs without the rest of these thieves, robbers, murderers, and outlaws knowing it, was more than he could conjure. His thoughts were interrupted by something happening near the bar.

"What's going on?" he hollered over.

"Looks like a couple of men left, Whitey. Probably goin' for horses and leavin' out. Probably have some of our gold in their poke, too."

"This ain't gonna be good. The only way we can get horses is to attack that livery as a group, carrying what little amount of gold we can. They ain't no other way," he was loud and angry. Those standing around, those that could actually think, knew he was right. The others couldn't see past the gold on the floor upstairs.

"I ain't leavin' that gold," one said. "No way."

"Fool," Whitey said. "You gonna drag a bag of gold, couple hundred pounds, over to the livery, fight off the damn townspeople, and steal a horse? If we don't think this through, we're all gonna die right here," he stormed.

"Somebody's coming out of the Red Rose Saloon," a man yelled from near the doorway. "Holding a white flag."

"Let's go hear what he has to say," Whitey said, limping toward the doors. "A couple of you stay back and keep us covered, just in case this is a trap."

"Maybe I'll just shoot the jasper anyway," somebody said, getting a growl from Whitey.

Leon and Whitey along with two others slipped out onto the street and advanced slowly toward Red Feather and Pete Quimby. "That's far enough," Red Feather said when the groups were separated by about thirty feet or so. He and Quimby had put themselves in such a position that a shot from the saloon would have to come very close to either Whitey or Leon.

"I'm New Mexico Territorial agent Jose Red Feather and this is my deputy and Plainsville Marshal Pete Quimby." Quimby had to hold in a smile at the mention of town marshal. That had not been brought up before. "You men are surrounded; you have no food or water, and no means of escape. Oh, yes, that side of beef we're roasting over there," and he pointed toward the livery, "is only for us. Smells delicious, doesn't it?

"Throw down you weapons and give yourselves up and you will live through this. Might even enjoy a roast beef dinner tonight. Fight us, and you will die. My citation is from the governor of the territory and you will be treated fairly. Give up now."

"I'd like to have a chance to talk to the men about that," Whitey said, believing what Red Feather said about being surrounded and out-gunned.

"You have half an hour," Red Feather said, turning, and he and Quimby walked back toward the Red Rose. As they entered, several gunshots erupted near the livery, and Whitey and Leon got back inside the Hearts of Gold Saloon as quickly as they could.

"Sounds like those jaspers that run out on us just got theirs," Leon said as they ducked into Holiday's saloon. "A few hours ago we had enough guns to take over this town, and look at us now. It looks like the only way out of here is gonna be on foot, Whitey."

Whitey spent the next ten minutes going over, again and again, what Red Feather had said. "Right now, I don't see any other way out of this. Without horses, where would we go? And, ain't no food or water in this hole. I ain't never give up in my life. Ever," he snarled, "but I just don't se no other way of stayin' alive."

A lot of men had a lot to say, and at the same time, nothing to say. "I think right now," Leon offered, "we're on our own. You want to fill your pockets with Holiday's gold and try to get out, go. You want to fight it out, wait until those that don't want to fight it out get out safely."

"What are you gonna do, Leon?" one of the men asked.

"I'm gonna walk out those doors, unarmed and with my hands up. I ain't killed nobody that they can prove, and I ain't behind all the Holiday crimes. At most get a couple of years, and be alive."

There were several, including Whitey shaking their heads in agreement, and a few others making their move for the stairway, to fill their pockets with as many gold coins as they could carry. "Ain't leavin' that gold," one said, "And to hell with you, Whitey."

Chapter Twenty-Two

J osh turned back toward Kirk Taylor, motioning that he could hear movement through the brush. Taylor had has rifle up, so did Joshua as two men from the Holiday saloon came up on the young man. Too quick for Josh to swing the rifle, one pulled his revolver, putting a slug through Pitts' leg. Taylor killed him instantly, and Josh, pain stabbing like wildfire, rolled free of the brush and shot the second man through his stomach.

"Bleeding heavy," Taylor muttered, running to Josh's side. "Hold still, son. Let me get this this rag tied on. Got to stop that bleeding." Bergstrom and Bill Pitts raced to them, and Bergstrom took control of the wounded outlaw. "Gotta get Josh inside and get that bleeding stopped," Taylor said, and he and Pitts lifted the boy up and ran toward the office.

Pitts had hold of his son's hand as Taylor ripped his boot off and tore his pants up the side of the leg, exposing a nasty wound to the thigh. "Right into the vein," Taylor muttered, applying pressure high on the inside of the thigh. "Come on, stop bleeding, Josh, damn it," he said, motioning for Bill Pitts to hold some rags tight to the wound. "That's the way. Stay with us Josh, you're gonna be fine," but he wasn't that sure that was the case.

Too many times I've watched good men bleed to death from what should be a simple wound to an arm or leg, he thought, pressing on the artery, watching the flow of blood slow to a trickle. "Get a good strong bandage tied over that wound, Bill," he said, "and then press hard on it." He could see that young Pitts was conscious, but just barely, smiled at him, and slowly eased off his pressure on the leg.

"It's holding," Bill Pitts said. "Is there any way we can get Doc Winters over here? He's half crippled, and those men in the saloon would shoot him on sight. We got to get that bullet out. Josh, son, stay with us," he said, tears racing down his weathered cheeks.

"This one's gone," Bergstrom said, dragging the body of the dead outlaw out of the office. "Gut shot. At least he went quick. Saw a man live four days after bein' gut shot," he muttered, coming back in. "I'm going back out where Taylor and Josh were. May be more of those fools tryin' for horses."

"While you were out back, Josh, Red Feather and Pete Quimby had a pow-wow with a couple of Holiday's men. After a couple of minutes, they turned and went back to the saloons. I think your plan to bring them out with a roasting side of beef is gonna work, son," he said, trying to smile, trying to keep Josh alive.

"He got too close, too fast," Josh murmured, grimacing with pain. "I'm sorry, Kirk."

"Sorry, my ass," Kirk Taylor snapped back. "Those two got on us quick, and it was you spotted 'em. You did fine, Josh, alerted me, got your man. If you hadn't heard them comin', we'd be the dead ones, and don't argue with me about that. You want me to smack that wound?" he said, bringing a soft laugh from the boy. "That's better."

Taylor spent the next half hour putting pressure on the artery, then releasing it, keeping a close eye on the bandage, holding tight to the wound. Pitts, beside himself with worry was starting to get Josh worked up when Taylor said it might be best if he went out to tend to the side of beef. "Make sure those boys are turning that beef, using those mops to put that good sauce on there. Don't want to lose that beef, Bill," he said. "Josh is gonna be fine. I'll yell if I need something."

One of the men from the spit crew popped in. "Something happening out on the street," he said, watching three men walk out of the Hearts of Gold Saloon. They stood on the sidewalk, undid their gun belts, letting them fall to the ground, and putting their hand in the air, walked slowly toward the Red Rose Saloon. Reynaldo Cortez and Pete Quimby met the three, and escorted them down the street to the jail. Before they got there, two more men came out of the Holiday saloon, dropped their weapons, and walked to a waiting Red Feather.

"How many left in there?" he asked one of the men, indicating they should walk down the middle of the street.

"Maybe three or four," he said. "They want to break out and run away on foot. They'd be comin' out those big barn doors."

At the jail, Red Feather motioned Pete to follow him. "Rey, keep things in order here. We'll probably be bringing some more people for you." As they turned to go out the door, Sloan showed up with the banker Henry Swanson in tow.

"Think he needs the company of some fine up-right citizens," Sloan smiled handing Swanson over to Cortez. "Coming to an end?" he asked, walking out of the jail with Red Feather and Quimby.

"I think so, Charlie," Pete Quimby said.

"Feller said about three or four more in the saloon, are filling their pockets with gold and plan to break out through those large barn doors. That's where we're heading." As they neared the Red Rose they saw Bill Pitts running toward Doc Winters place.

"Now what?" Sloan asked. The three changed direction and met Pitts and Doc. "What happened?" Charlie asked, as Pitts helped Doc walk a little faster than he wanted to.

"They shot Josh," Pitts stammered. "He's been bleeding real heavy."

"I'll help you with the doc," Sloan said, taking Winters' arm. "You boys go wipe out that gang of rattlesnakes. I'll join you when doc gets workin'." With his size and strength, Sloan was able to get doc moving along at a good pace, actually slowing Pitts down a bit. "Glad to see you, Doc," he smiled. Winters nodded a gracious 'thank you.'

***

Four men were in Holiday's office, stuffing gold coins in their pockets, almost salivating at the thought of that much money being available for the taking. "I can't get no more in," one said, and started for the stairway, the others right along with him. "Kill those jaspers at the stables, saddle some good horses, and head for Texas," the large outlaw said, leaving a trail of gold coins spilling from his pockets.

"Not me. I'm heading for Mexico and build me a good place to work from. Lots of banks along the border," another said as the group descended into the saloon's storage cellar. They moved up the ramp on the other side of the large room, toward the large barn doors. The smaller man-door was standing ajar and one of the men took a peek outside.

"Don't see nobody," he said, looking all around. "Can't see nobody over by them corrals either. Let's go," and he snuck out the door, bent over, running for some heavy brush on the other side of the cottonwoods. The other three were right behind him when Red Feather and Pete Quimby stepped out from the brush, rifles in hand.

"Hold it right there," Red Feather hollered, leveling the rifle at the lead man. "Stop, drop your weapons, and you will live. I won't say it again," and the first man stopped. The others tried to dodge behind the cottonwood trees. Quimby's rifle barked twice and two men fell face first in the dirt, cold coins erupting from their pockets.

Red Feather turned and shot the third man and immediately turned back, his rifle aimed at the stopped outlaw's head. "Don't do it," he snarled, watching the man's hand slowly move toward his holstered revolver. "Put your hands high over your head," Red Feather said as Pete Quimby walked toward the man to disarm him.

"Careful, Pete. He's not thinking," and the man made a play for his gun, never feeling the rifle slug that entered his head, directly between his eyes. "Idiot," is all Red Feather said.

The gunfire emptied the livery stables and Red Rose Saloon. Men with rifles came from behind Holiday's place, from around the corrals, and down the main street of Plainsville, first spotting Red Feather and Quimby standing over the dead outlaws, then seeing the gold coins scattered on the ground and leaking from pockets.

"Would you look at that," Rose Flannigan said, pointing at the coins. "I've got to get inside, Pete. Help me find Gerald. Oh, god, I hope he made it. That poor man," she said, walking toward the saloon.

"Wait, Rose," Quimby said, taking her arm. "We don't know if there's no one in there." Reynaldo Cortez loped down from the jail after hearing the shots and seeing all the action, and Pete motioned for him to come with him. "We need to make sure that saloon is empty and see if we can find Gerald Sorenson. It's not safe, Rose. Let us do it," he said.

The Irish temper flared briefly as she demanded that she accompany them in their search. "Can't fight her, Pete," Rey chuckled, and with Pete just shaking his head, the three walked toward the bat-wing doors of the Hearts of Gold Saloon.

***

Chaos is what they found inside the saloon, bottles strewn about, tables and chairs turned over, and a stream of gold coins leading up the grand staircase to Holiday's office. It took a full five minutes of intense searching to find Gerald Sorenson's body, stuffed behind a piano, as a filthy old rag might have been.

"Oh, Gerald," Rose cried. "I'm so sorry. It must have been horrid. Those foul men," she stormed. "All of them should hang, twice. Gerald," she moaned, sinking into

Reynaldo's arms. "He was so kind to everyone, took such good care of the hotel and our guests. Hang those bastards," she said softly, allowing Cortez to ease her out of the horrific scene.

"Let's spread the word through the town," Quimby said as they joined the others in the street. "Let them know their town is safe, and I'd like to get as many people as possible to come to the stables. Everybody, spread out, go door to door, let's have our Fourth of July, Independence Day party a little early this year. There's a large, tender beef roasting to perfection, we have good wine and whiskey, compliments of Thornton Holiday, and the Plainsville treasury actually exists, again, thanks to Mr. Holiday."

A cheer when up from those around Quimby and Charlie Sloan walked up, grabbed the big man and gave him a bear hug, lifting his feet right off the ground. "Well done, Pete," is all he said, and shook his hand vigorously. The two stood looking at each other for a couple of minutes, understanding that their little piece of paradise had withstood the challenge.

"Let's get these bodies buried, Charlie, and then see if we can get some kind of party underway." They gathered up several men with picks and shovels, had other men search and gather the dead, and performed dutiful but quick services.

Rose spoke briefly as they tucked little Gerald Sorenson into his grave, holding onto Rey Cortez as tightly as she could. "You were a dear friend, Gerald. Sleep in peace, my friend."

***

It was a raucous night in Plainsville. Led by Rose Flannigan, many of the women quickly prepared side dishes to be served with the spit roasted side of beef. Sawhorses had been spaced about on the main street with planking on top to make tables, tableware was provided by the café, and libations from the Hearts of Gold.

Quimby spoke of the future of Plainsville, how the city would incorporate, with territorial blessing, and grow as the railroad spur was brought in. All of his southern background flowed through his speech, his sonorous voice echoing from the buildings. Red Feather spoke of law and order, good citizenship, and that a belief in individual responsibility would make Plainsville a wonderful place to live, raise a family, and prosper.

As great slabs of beef were brought to the table, after all the oratory was over, and mouths were watering having enjoyed the aroma for a couple of hours, Bill Pitts, Sonny Bergstrom, and Kirk Taylor came out of the livery office, carrying Joshua Pitts on a homemade litter, bringing him right up to the table. "Here is the real hero," Kirk Taylor said. "Without this young man's knowledge of the town and the people, and without his brazen plan to wipe out the Holiday Gang, that is, this wonderful side of beef, Holiday and company would still be running things.

"To you, Josh Pitts, one damn fine horseman, one damn fine young man," and the crowd stood and cheered. Josh turned purple with embarrassment, had a little boy grin on his face, and full rivers of tears splashing down his cheeks. Bill Pitts, with just as many tears, hugged his son, clapped him on the back, and just stood in silence before the crowd, unable to say a word.

Reynaldo Cortez brought everyone back to reality, simply saying, "let's eat," and the crowd formed a line to fill plates with roast beef, steamed vegetables, roasted potatoes, and glasses of whatever suited them. The feast lasted deep into the night, and more than one person brought musical instruments. There was fiddle and banjo music, community singing, and one of Peterson's cowboys brought out his harmonica and danced a jig as he played.

Holiday would have been incensed at the amount of his liquor that had been consumed. "How much gold do you suppose there was in that hoard upstairs?" Sloan asked Quimby, as things slowly settled down.

"It'll take several days to get it all sorted out, I think. We got it moved into the vault at the bank, and found even more gold stashed there. Plainsville will come into existence with a poke full, I'm thinking," he smiled, laughing along with Charlie Sloan.

"First thing in the morning, now that Red Feather has given me the title of Marshal, I'm going to set up a schedule of meetings, and by this time next week, we will actually exist as a town, and will have our petition for incorporation on its way to Santa Fé and the governor.

"We did it, Charlie. We did it."

***

Reynaldo was helping Rose Flannigan with cleanup, as the town people slowly headed back to their homes. "One fine party," Rose said, letting the big ranch hand slip his arm around her waist. "I'm so sorry for Gerald, and I'm so happy for Josh, and I think I'm going to cry again," she sobbed, as Cortez drew her in tight.

"I think I'm going to give you something to cry about, Mrs. Rose Flannigan," he said, tilting her chin up, smiling into those blazing Irish eyes. "The only thing I have to offer, dear lady, is a strong body, a sound mind, and undying love. Will you marry me?"

Chapter Twenty-Three

T he banner spread across the dusty main street, proclaiming to one and all, "Welcome to Plainsville, New Mexico Territory." Under the banner stood a platform, with chairs for dignitaries, and a podium for speakers. Most of the two hundred residents of Plainsville and the surrounding ranches were either on the platform or spread out across the street, ready for the presentation.

All the businesses were closed with the exception of the Red Rose Saloon, but the only person in there was Old Pete, calmly walking back and forth behind the bar, wiping down unseen stains and spills, and waiting for the dignitaries to get through with their part of the day, so he could do his part.

Pete Quimby stood up and walked to the podium. He wore neatly pressed trousers, a blazing white shirt with ornate string tie, and a tin badge declaring him "Marshal." He stood at the podium, a broad smile across his face.

"As most of you know, I love to talk," and there were guffaws, even friendly cat-calls at that statement, "but today, so special to so many of us, is a day for others to talk. He's on a tight schedule, due back in the capitol for some important legislation, so we now welcome to Plainsville, the governor of New Mexico Territory, James P. Monahan. Mr. Governor?"

To extended applause, the governor stood, bowed slightly to Rose, then to Quimby, and made his way to the podium. "This is one of the proudest moments of my tenure as your governor," he started. "There were many doubts that Plainsville would survive the horrific onslaught by those outlaws, but it is because many believed in the town, in themselves, and in the spirit of the rule of law, that today is here.

"Mark your calendars for future celebrations. June

10 will always be known as Plainsville Day. Yes, the Legislature passed the measure you asked for, and I have signed the incorporation papers naming this a legal and lawful township in New Mexico Territory."

The crowd erupted, cheering, whistling, yes, even excited gunfire, and Governor Monahan allowed it to go on for several minutes, finally waving his hands for quiet. "None of this would have happened if it weren't for one person, the former Rose Flannigan, now known, territory wide as Rose Cortez," and he motioned for Rose to stand, and the crowd roared its approval.

"You have created a town, you have elected city officials, and you have been accepted by the governing body. Now, make the town prosperous, make yourselves prosperous. You have fought off the evil, relish now, the fruits of your labor. I must leave you now, but know in your hearts how proud I am of every single one of you." The crowd cheered for many minutes as the governor made his way to his carriage, to be escorted back to Santa Fé by Red Feather and two deputies.

Quimby moved back to the podium as the crowd settled down a bit. "It's time to introduce our town officials," he said, glancing behind him to make sure everyone was there. "Kirk Taylor has become cow boss at the former Peterson Ranch, now owned by the cowboys that worked for Dave, is now Mayor of Plainsville, and has opted to not give a speech." The crowd cheered, then demanded Kirk come to the podium.

"I'm not a speech-a-fier," he said, swallowing hard, "but I will tell you this. I will work as hard as it is possible to make you proud to live in Plainsville." He bowed slightly to Pete Quimby, waved his big black sombrero to the crowd and went back to his seat, to a long cheer.

"For the time being," Quimby said, "I'll be the law," flipping his badge with his thumb, "but we will be electing a sheriff next month. I'm very proud to tell you that Bill Pitts has accepted the position of Town Judge, and will be holding court every Tuesday and Friday." He took the moments while cheering was going on to glance at Rose, giving her a big smile.

"There is one person the governor neglected to mention in his speech, and without the brilliant thinking of Josh Pitts, Plainsville probably wouldn't be here right now. He's too young in years, not ability or spirit, to serve as an elected official, so in my non-official capacity of host on this first town-wide celebration, I am naming future annual celebrations as Josh Pitts Day."

There wasn't a quiet voice in the town as Quimby helped the still partially crippled young man to the podium. All Josh could do was wave at the crowd, smile so broadly it probably hurt, and let the tears flow. He tried to say something, found he had no voice, waved again, and sat down.

"He's the bravest young man Plainsville has ever known," Quimby said, letting the crowd settle down again. "Before this all ends," he said. "There is one more person that needs to be heard, probably the most important speech we will hear today.

"I'm honored to introduce the vice president of operations of the Santa Fé Railroad, Mr. Ralph Flowers." Flowers, in full business dress, including boat-tail coat, walked to the podium, a broad smile across his weathered face.

"It's been a hell of a fight, Quimby, Rose, but you have won it, and won it well. I'm only going to make this one statement, then we can retire to cooler areas of town, like the Red Rose Saloon, to continue the celebration. The surveys have been completed, work has begun, and the Plainsville spur will see its first locomotive moving before the Fourth of July."

He clapped his hand, waved his top hat, and helped the town cheer for a full five minutes. He joined Rose,

Reynaldo, and Pete Quimby at the bar. "Without you, Rose, we wouldn't be here. Pete, you did a fine job. We'll have a long association. And, you, Mr. Cortez, sir, you take care of this lady."

His toast to them over, he left for the long buggy ride back to the capitol. Rose looked long and hard at Pete. "As you said the other day, Pete. We did it, pal. We did it."

About the Author:

I've had a wonderful and varied time along this bumpy highway called life. I spent my early years in Santa Cruz, California, swimming, fishing, and wallowing in the splendor of redwoods, the Monterey Bay, and a loving family. Then, my four years of high school were spent living on the Island of Guam. That was back in the early 1950s Yes, Virginia, I am that old, but only in body, not spirit.

My first job in radio was in 1958. I bought the Virginia City Legend newspaper in that old western mining community in 1971, and retired from having a job in 2010. That's when I changed from being a reporter of news to being a writer of fiction, and over these last few years have found my western and crime/mystery stories published as novels and in magazines and anthologies, around the world.

I'm a proud member of The Western Fictioneers, the organization for professional authors of Western novels and short stories.

My beautiful wife Patty and I live on a small hobby farm about twenty miles north of Reno, Nevada, sharing space with a couple of fine horses, a flock of egg-producing chickens, and some breeding rabbits. You're always welcome to visit. I need help cleaning those corrals.

Social Media Links:

Facebook: https://www.facebook.com/johnny.gunn.31

Blog: http://johnny-gunn.blogspot.com/

Twitter: https://twitter.com/johnnygunn11

Jacob Chance, U.S. Marshal

Land law, water rights, deeds of ownership? Boring. Unless of course, people are shooting at you because of them. The Civil War has disrupted thousands of lives, including that of Sarah Jackson, whose husband was killed for not joining the Confederate Army in Georgia. Sarah and her daughter flee to Nevada Territory and are eligible for homestead rights. After claiming her one hundred sixty acres in the lush Golden Valley, her world crumbles again.

Banker Preston Miller claims he owns the entire Golden Valley and all the water in the Good Hope River. Jackson cries foul in a letter to the U.S. Attorney in San Francisco, and Jacob Chance, U.S. Marshal rides to Preston, Nevada Territory to "settle this little land dispute."

He finds many in the town fear for their lives and livelihood, but it takes just a few shots from big guns to convince them to back the marshal. Lives are lost, buildings are burned, the town itself is in jeopardy, and the U.S. Marshal finds himself up against an army. Anarchy is the rule in the Golden Valley.

Fighting the bad guys is hard enough, he also finds himself fascinated by the daughter of one of the ranchers whose property he is trying to save. Will the town survive? Will the ranches survive? Is romance in the air? All the answers are inside these covers.

The Quest

Tom Henry, a writer, amateur archaeologist, and historian, is confronted one hot summer day by what he can only describe as a time and space traveler. He fears for his sanity as he is introduced to what the ancient people of the deserts of Nevada used as areas of intense energy for shamans to travel between realities. His guide is Riba, a Quarian, a dominant species in the universe, who introduces him to time and space travel by way of mind power only. Beware, Tom fears that Riba is more than a guide. Beware, you might be drawn into this great unknown.

Paradise Challenged

Thornton Holiday is a murderer, a bank robber, and a man with a plan, a plan to create an outlaw haven in the New Mexico Territory community of Plainsville. He's mad with power, one might say, 'his ego runneth over.' The village is overrun with the meanest outlaws in the west, ranchers and local businessmen are killed, and election fraud allows a murderer to become sheriff.

The Plainsville citizens plea with the governor for help and a special territorial agent is called on. He appoints a leading town figure to be his deputy and the town fights back. It takes the wit and wisdom of a fourteen-year-old boy who demands to be considered a man, to come up a plan to root out the outlaw element. It's gold the outlaws want but Josh Pitts knows something else they might hunger for.